MARRIAGE

H. G. WELLS

BOOK THE FIRST

MARJORIE MARRIES

CHAPTER THE FIRST

A Day with the Popes

§ 1

An extremely pretty girl occupied a second-class compartment in one of those trains which percolate through the rural tranquillities of middle England from Ganford in Oxfordshire to Rumbold Junction in Kent. She was going to join her family at Buryhamstreet after a visit to some Gloucestershire friends. Her father, Mr. Pope, once a leader in the coach-building world and now by retirement a gentleman, had taken the Buryhamstreet vicarage furnished for two months (beginning on the fifteenth of July) at his maximum summer rental of seven guineas a week. His daughter was on her way to this retreat.

At first she had been an animated traveller, erect and keenly regardful of every detail upon the platforms of the stations at which her conveyance lingered, but the tedium of the journey and the warmth of the sunny afternoon had relaxed her pose by imperceptible degrees, and she sat now comfortably in the corner, with her neat toes upon the seat before her, ready to drop them primly at the first sign of a fellow-traveller. Her expression lapsed more and more towards an almost somnolent reverie. She wished she had not taken a second-class ticket, because then she might have afforded a cup of tea at Reading, and so fortified herself against this insinuating indolence.

She was travelling second class, instead of third as she ought to have done, through one of those lapses so inevitable to young people in her position. The two Carmel boys and a cousin, two greyhounds and a chow had come to see her off; they had made a brilliant and prosperous group on the platform and extorted the manifest admiration of two youthful porters, and it had been altogether too much for Marjorie Pope to admit it was the family custom—except when her father's nerves had to be considered—to go third class. So she had made a hasty calculation—she knew her balance to a penny because of the recent tipping—and found it would just run to it. Fourpence remained,—and there would be a porter at Buryhamstreet!

Her mother had said: "You will have Ample." Well, opinions of amplitude vary. With numerous details fresh in her mind, Marjorie decided it would be wiser to avoid financial discussion during her first few days at Buryhamstreet.

There was much in Marjorie's equipment in the key of travelling second class at the sacrifice of afternoon tea. There was, for example, a certain quiet goodness of style about her clothes, though the skirt betrayed age, and an entire absence of style about her luggage, which was all in the compartment with her, and which consisted of a distended hold-all, a very good tennis racquet in a stretcher, a portmanteau of cheap white basketwork held together by straps, and a very new, expensive-looking and meretricious dressing-bag of imitation morocco, which had been one of her chief financial errors at Oxbridge. The collection was eloquent indeed of incompatible standards....

Marjorie had a chin that was small in size if resolute in form, and a mouth that was not noticeably soft and weak because it was conspicuously soft and pretty. Her nose was delicately aquiline and very subtly and finely modelled, and she looked out upon the world with steady, grey-blue eyes beneath broad, level brows that contradicted in a large measure the hint of weakness below. She had an abundance of copper-red hair, which flowed back very prettily from her broad, low forehead and over her delicate ears, and she had that warm-tinted clear skin that goes so well with reddish hair. She had a very dainty neck, and the long slender lines of her body were full of the promise of a riper beauty. She had the good open shoulders of a tennis-player and a swimmer. Some day she was to be a tall, ruddy, beautiful woman. She wore simple clothes of silvery grey and soft green, and about her waist was a belt of grey leather in which there now wilted two creamy-petalled roses.

That was the visible Marjorie. Somewhere out of time and space was an invisible Marjorie who looked out on the world with those steady eyes, and smiled or drooped with the soft red lips, and dreamt, and wondered, and desired.

<h3 style="text-align:center">§ 2</h3>

What a queer thing the invisible human being would appear if, by some discovery as yet inconceivable, some spiritual X-ray photography, we could flash it into sight! Long ago I read a book called "Soul Shapes" that was full of ingenious ideas, but I doubt very much if the thing so revealed would have any shape, any abiding solid outline at all. It is something more fluctuating and discursive than that—at any rate, for every one young enough not to have set and hardened. Things come into it and become it, things drift out of it and cease to be it, things turn upside down in it and change and colour and dissolve, and grow and eddy about and blend into each other. One might figure it, I suppose, as a preposterous jumble animated by a will; a floundering disconnectedness through which an old hump of impulse rises and thrusts unaccountably; a river beast of purpose wallowing in a back eddy of mud and weeds and floating objects and creatures drowned. Now the sunshine of gladness makes it all vivid, now it is sombre and grimly insistent under the sky of some darkling mood, now an emotional gale sweeps across it and it is one confused agitation....

And surely these invisible selves of men were never so jumbled, so crowded, complicated, and stirred about as they are at the present time. Once I am told they had a sort of order, were sphered in religious beliefs, crystal clear, were arranged in a cosmogony that fitted them as hand fits glove, were separated by definite standards of right and wrong which presented life as planned in all its essential aspects from the cradle to the grave. Things are so no longer. That sphere is broken for most of us; even if it is tied about and mended again, it is burst like a seed case; things have fallen out and things have fallen in....

Can I convey in any measure how it was with Marjorie?

What was her religion?

In college forms and returns, and suchlike documents, she would describe herself as "Church of England." She had been baptized according to the usages of that body, but she had hitherto evaded confirmation into it, and although it is a large, wealthy, and powerful organization with many minds to serve it, it had never succeeded in getting into her quick and apprehensive intelligence any lucid and persuasive conception of what it considered God and the universe were up to with her. It had failed to catch her attention and state itself to her. A number of humorous and other writers and the general trend of talk around her, and perhaps her own shrewd little observation of superficial things, had, on the other hand, created a fairly definite belief in her that it wasn't as a matter of fact up to very much at all, that what it said wasn't said with that absolute honesty which is a logical necessity in every religious authority, and that its hierarchy had all sorts of political and social considerations confusing its treatment of her immortal soul....

Marjorie followed her father in abstaining from church. He too professed himself

"Church of England," but he was, if we are to set aside merely superficial classifications, an irascible atheist with a respect for usage and Good Taste, and an abject fear of the disapproval of other gentlemen of his class. For the rest he secretly disliked clergymen on account of the peculiarity of their collars, and a certain influence they had with women. When Marjorie at the age of fourteen had displayed a hankering after ecclesiastical ceremony and emotional religion, he had declared: "We don't want any of that nonsense," and sent her into the country to a farm where there were young calves and a bottle-fed lamb and kittens. At times her mother went to church and displayed considerable orthodoxy and punctilio, at times the good lady didn't, and at times she thought in a broad-minded way that there was a Lot in Christian Science, and subjected herself to the ministrations of an American named Silas Root. But his ministrations were too expensive for continuous use, and so the old faith did not lose its hold upon the family altogether.

At school Marjorie had been taught what I may best describe as Muffled Christianity—a temperate and discreet system designed primarily not to irritate parents, in which the painful symbol of the crucifixion and the riddle of what Salvation was to save her from, and, indeed, the coarser aspects of religion generally, were entirely subordinate to images of amiable perambulations, and a rich mist of finer feelings. She had been shielded, not only from arguments against her religion, but from arguments for it—the two things go together—and I do not think it was particularly her fault if she was now growing up like the great majority of respectable English people, with her religious faculty as it were, artificially faded, and an acquired disposition to regard any speculation of why she was, and whence and whither, as rather foolish, not very important, and in the very worst possible taste.

And so, the crystal globe being broken which once held souls together, you may expect to find her a little dispersed and inconsistent in her motives, and with none of that assurance a simpler age possessed of the exact specification of goodness or badness, the exact delimitation of right and wrong. Indeed, she did not live in a world of right and wrong, or anything so stern; "horrid" and "jolly" had replaced these archaic orientations. In a world where a mercantile gentility has conquered passion and God is neither blasphemed nor adored, there necessarily arises this generation of young people, a little perplexed, indeed, and with a sense of something missing, but feeling their way inevitably at last to the great releasing question, "Then why shouldn't we have a good time?"

Yet there was something in Marjorie, as in most human beings, that demanded some general idea, some aim, to hold her life together. A girl upon the borders of her set at college was fond of the phrase "living for the moment," and Marjorie associated with it the speaker's lax mouth, sloe-like eyes, soft, quick-flushing, boneless face, and a habit of squawking and bouncing in a forced and graceless manner. Marjorie's natural disposition was to deal with life in a steadier spirit than that. Yet all sorts of powers and forces were at work in her, some exalted, some elvish, some vulgar, some subtle. She felt keenly and desired strongly, and in effect she came perhaps nearer the realization of that offending phrase than its original exponent. She had a clean intensity of feeling that made her delight in a thousand various things, in sunlight and textures, and the vividly quick acts of animals, in landscape, and the beauty of other girls, in wit, and people's voices, and good strong reasoning, and the desire and skill of art. She had a clear, rapid memory that made her excel perhaps a little too easily at school and college, an eagerness of sympathetic interest that won people very quickly and led to disappointments, and a very strong sense of the primary importance of Miss Marjorie Pope in the world. And when any very definite dream of what she would like to be and what she would like to do, such as being the principal of a ladies' college, or the first woman member of Parliament, or the wife of a barbaric chief in Borneo, or a great explorer, or the wife of a millionaire and a great social leader, or George Sand, or Saint Teresa, had had possession of her imagination for a few weeks, an entirely contrasted and equally attractive dream would presently arise beside it and compete with it and replace it. It wasn't so much that she turned against the old one as that she was attracted by the new, and she forgot the old dream rather than abandoned it, simply because she was only one person, and hadn't therefore the possibility of realizing both.

In certain types Marjorie's impressionability aroused a passion of proselytism. People of the most diverse kinds sought to influence her, and they invariably did so. Quite a number of people, including her mother and the principal of her college, believed themselves to be the leading influence in her life. And this was particularly the case with her aunt Plessington. Her aunt Plessington was devoted to social and political work of an austere and aggressive sort (in which Mr. Plessington participated); she was childless, and had a Movement of her own, the Good Habits Movement, a progressive movement of the utmost scope and benevolence which aimed at extensive interferences with the food and domestic intimacies of the more defenceless lower classes by means ultimately of legislation, and she had Marjorie up to see her, took her for long walks while she influenced with earnestness and vigour, and at times had an air of bequeathing her mantle, movement and everything, quite definitely to her "little Madge." She spoke of training her niece to succeed her, and bought all the novels of Mrs. Humphry Ward for her as they appeared, in the hope of quickening in her that flame of politico-social ambition, that insatiable craving for dinner-parties with important guests, which is so distinctive of the more influential variety of English womanhood. It was due rather to her own habit of monologue than to any reserve on the part of Marjorie that she entertained the belief that her niece was entirely acquiescent in these projects.

They went into Marjorie's mind and passed. For nearly a week, it is true, she had dramatized herself as the angel and inspiration of some great modern statesman, but this had been ousted by a far more insistent dream, begotten by a picture she had seen in some exhibition, of a life of careless savagery, whose central and constantly recurrent incident was the riding of barebacked horses out of deep-shadowed forest into a foamy sunlit sea—in a costume that would certainly have struck Aunt Plessington as a mistake.

If you could have seen Marjorie in her railway compartment, with the sunshine, sunshine mottled by the dirty window, tangled in her hair and creeping to and fro over her face as the train followed the curves of the line, you would certainly have agreed with me that she was pretty, and you might even have thought her beautiful. But it was necessary to fall in love with Marjorie before you could find her absolutely beautiful. You might have speculated just what business was going on behind those drowsily thoughtful eyes. If you are—as people say—"Victorian," you might even have whispered "Day Dreams," at the sight of her....

She was dreaming, and in a sense she was thinking of beautiful things. But only mediately. She was thinking how very much she would enjoy spending freely and vigorously, quite a considerable amount of money,—heaps of money.

You see, the Carmels, with whom she had just been staying, were shockingly well off. They had two motor cars with them in the country, and the boys had the use of the second one as though it was just an old bicycle. Marjorie had had a cheap white dinner-dress, made the year before by a Chelsea French girl, a happy find of her mother's, and it was shapely and simple and not at all bad, and she had worn her green beads and her Egyptian necklace of jade; but Kitty Carmel and her sister had had a new costume nearly every night, and pretty bracelets, and rubies, big pearls, and woven gold, and half a score of delightful and precious things for neck and hair. Everything in the place was bright and good and abundant, the servants were easy and well-mannered, without a trace of hurry or resentment, and one didn't have to be sharp about the eggs and things at breakfast in the morning, or go without. All through the day, and even when they had gone to bathe from the smart little white and green shed on the upper lake, Marjorie had been made to feel the insufficiency of her equipment. Kitty Carmel, being twenty-one, possessed her own cheque-book and had accounts running at half a dozen West-end shops; and both sisters had furnished their own rooms according to their taste, with a sense of obvious effect that had set Marjorie speculating just how a room might be done by a girl with a real eye for colour and a real brain behind it....

The train slowed down for the seventeenth time. Marjorie looked up and read "Buryhamstreet."

§ 3

Her reverie vanished, and by a complex but almost instantaneous movement she had her basket off the rack and the carriage door open. She became teeming anticipations. There, advancing in a string, were Daffy, her elder sister, Theodore, her younger brother, and the dog Toupee. Sydney and Rom hadn't come. Daffy was not copper red like her sister, but really quite coarsely red-haired; she was bigger than Marjorie, and with irregular teeth instead of Marjorie's neat row; she confessed them in a broad simple smile of welcome. Theodore was hatless, rustily fuzzy-headed, and now a wealth of quasi-humorous gesture. The dog Toupee was straining at a leash, and doing its best in a yapping, confused manner, to welcome the wrong people by getting its lead round their legs.

"Toupee!" cried Marjorie, waving the basket. "Toupee!"

They all called it Toupee because it was like one, but the name was forbidden in her father's hearing. Her father had decided that the proper name for a family dog in England is Towser, and did his utmost to suppress a sobriquet that was at once unprecedented and not in the best possible taste. Which was why the whole family, with the exception of Mrs. Pope, of course, stuck to Toupee....

Marjorie flashed a second's contrast with the Carmel splendours.

"Hullo, old Daffy. What's it like?" she asked, handing out the basket as her sister came up.

"It's a lark," said Daffy. "Where's the dressing-bag?"

"Thoddy," said Marjorie, following up the dressing-bag with the hold-all. "Lend a hand."

"Stow it, Toupee," said Theodore, and caught the hold-all in time.

In another moment Marjorie was out of the train, had done the swift kissing proper to the occasion, and rolled a hand over Toupee's head—Toupee, who, after a passionate lunge at a particularly savoury drover from the next compartment, was now frantically trying to indicate that Marjorie was the one human being he had ever cared for. Brother and sister were both sketching out the state of affairs at Buryhamstreet Vicarage in rapid competitive jerks, each eager to tell things first—and the whole party moved confusedly towards the station exit. Things pelted into Marjorie's mind.

"We've got an old donkey-cart. I thought we shouldn't get here—ever.... Madge, we can go up the church tower whenever we like, only old Daffy won't let me shin up the flagstaff. It's perfectly safe—you couldn't fall off if you tried.... Had positively to get out at the level crossing and pull him over.... There's a sort of moat in the garden.... You never saw such furniture, Madge! And the study! It's hung with texts, and stuffed with books about the Scarlet Woman.... Piano's rather good, it's a Broadwood.... The Dad's got a war on about the tennis net. Oh, frightful! You'll see. It won't keep up. He's had a letter kept waiting by the Times for a fortnight, and it's a terror at breakfast. Says the motor people have used influence to silence him. Says that's a game two can play at.... Old Sid got herself upset stuffing windfalls. Rather a sell for old Sid, considering how refined she's getting...."

There was a brief lull as the party got into the waiting governess cart. Toupee, after a preliminary refusal to enter, made a determined attempt on the best seat, from which he would be able to bark in a persistent, official manner at anything that passed. That suppressed, and Theodore's proposal to drive refused, they were able to start, and attention was concentrated upon Daffy's negotiation of the station approach. Marjorie turned on her brother with a smile of warm affection.

"How are you, old Theodore?"

"I'm all right, old Madge."

"Mummy?"

"Every one's all right," said Theodore; "if it wasn't for that damned infernal net——"

"Ssssh!" cried both sisters together.

"He says it," said Theodore.

Both sisters conveyed a grave and relentless disapproval.

"Pretty bit of road," said Marjorie. "I like that little house at the corner."

A pause and the eyes of the sisters met.

"He's here," said Daffy.

Marjorie affected ignorance.

"Who's here?"

"Il vostro senior Miraculoso."

"Just as though a fellow couldn't understand your kiddy little Italian," said Theodore, pulling Toupee's ear.

"Oh well, I thought he might be," said Marjorie, regardless of her brother.

"Oh!" said Daffy. "I didn't know——"

Both sisters looked at each other, and then both glanced at Theodore. He met Marjorie's eyes with a grimace of profound solemnity.

"Little brothers," he said, "shouldn't know. Just as though they didn't! Rot! But let's change the subject, my dears, all the same. Lemme see. There are a new sort of flea on Toupee, Madge, that he gets from the hens."

"Is a new sort," corrected Daffy. "He's horrider than ever, Madge. He leaves his soap in soak now to make us think he has used it. This is the village High Street. Isn't it jolly?"

"Corners don't bite people," said Theodore, with a critical eye to the driving.

Marjorie surveyed the High Street, while Daffy devoted a few moments to Theodore.

The particular success of the village was its brace of chestnut trees which, with that noble disregard of triteness which is one of the charms of villages the whole world over, shadowed the village smithy. On either side of the roadway between it and the paths was a careless width of vivid grass protected by white posts, which gave way to admit a generous access on either hand to a jolly public house, leering over red blinds, and swinging a painted sign against its competitor. Several of the cottages had real thatch and most had porches; they had creepers nailed to their faces, and their gardens, crowded now with flowers, marigolds, begonias, snapdragon, delphiniums, white foxgloves, and monkshood, seemed almost too good to be true. The doctor's house was pleasantly Georgian, and the village shop, which was also a post and telegraph office, lay back with a slight air of repletion, keeping its bulging double shop-windows wide open in a manifest attempt not to fall asleep. Two score of shock-headed boys and pinafored girls were drilling upon a bald space of ground before the village school, and near by, the national emotion at the ever-memorable Diamond Jubilee of Queen Victoria had evoked an artistic drinking-fountain of grey stone. Beyond the subsequent green—there were the correctest geese thereon—the village narrowed almost to a normal road again, and then, recalling itself with a start, lifted a little to the churchyard wall about the grey and ample church. "It's just like all the villages that ever were," said Marjorie, and gave a cry of delight when Daffy, pointing to the white gate between two elm trees that led to the vicarage, remarked: "That's us."

In confirmation of which statement, Sydney and Rom, the two sisters next in succession to Marjorie, and with a strong tendency to be twins in spite of the year between them, appeared in a state of vociferous incivility opening the way for the donkey-carriage. Sydney was Sydney, and Rom was just short for Romola—one of her mother's favourite heroines in fiction.

"Old Madge," they said; and then throwing respect to the winds, "Old Gargoo!" which was Marjorie's forbidden nickname, and short for gargoyle (though surely only Victorian Gothic, ever produced a gargoyle that had the remotest right to be associated with the neat brightness of Marjorie's face).

She overlooked the offence, and the pseudo-twins boarded the cart from behind, whereupon the already overburthened donkey, being old and in a manner wise, quickened his pace for the house to get the whole thing over.

"It's really an avenue," said Daffy; but Marjorie, with her mind strung up to the Carmel standards, couldn't agree. It was like calling a row of boy-scouts Potsdam grenadiers. The trees were at irregular distances, of various ages, and mostly on one side. Still it was a shady, pleasant approach.

And the vicarage was truly very interesting and amusing. To these Londoners accustomed to live in a state of compression, elbows practically touching, in a tall, narrow fore-and-aft stucco house, all window and staircase, in a despondent Brompton square, there was an effect of maundering freedom about the place, of enlargement almost to the pitch of adventure and sunlight to the pitch of intoxication. The house itself was long and low, as if a London house holidaying in the country had flung itself asprawl; it had two disconnected and roomy staircases, and when it had exhausted itself completely as a house, it turned to the right and began again as rambling, empty stables, coach house, cart sheds, men's bedrooms up ladders, and outhouses of the most various kinds.

On one hand was a neglected orchard, in the front of the house was a bald, worried-looking lawn area capable of simultaneous tennis and croquet, and at the other side a copious and confused vegetable and flower garden full of roses, honesty, hollyhocks, and suchlike herbaceous biennials and perennials, lapsed at last into shrubbery, where a sickle-shaped, weedy lagoon of uncertain aims, which had evidently, as a rustic bridge and a weeping willow confessed, aspired to be an "ornamental water," declined at last to ducks. And there was access to the church, and the key of the church tower, and one went across the corner of the lawn, and by a little iron gate into the churchyard to decipher inscriptions, as if the tombs of all Buryhamstreet were no more than a part of the accommodation relinquished by the vicar's household.

Marjorie was hurried over the chief points of all this at a breakneck pace by Sydney and Rom, and when Sydney was called away to the horrors of practice—for Sydney in spite of considerable reluctance was destined by her father to be "the musical one"—Rom developed a copious affection, due apparently to some occult æsthetic influence in Marjorie's silvery-grey and green, and led her into the unlocked vestry, and there prayed in a whisper that she might be given "one good hug, just one"—and so they came out with their arms about each other very affectionately to visit the lagoon again. And then Rom remembered that Marjorie hadn't seen either the walnut-tree in the orchard, or the hen with nine chicks....

Somewhere among all these interests came tea and Mrs. Pope.

Mrs. Pope kissed her daughter with an air of having really wanted to kiss her half an hour ago, but of having been distracted since. She was a fine-featured, anxious-looking little woman, with a close resemblance to all her children, in spite of the fact that they were markedly dissimilar one to the other, except only that they took their ruddy colourings from their father. She was dressed in a neat blue dress that had perhaps been hurriedly chosen, and her method of doing her hair was a manifest compromise between duty and pleasure. She embarked at once upon an exposition of the bedroom arrangements, which evidently involved difficult issues. Marjorie was to share a room with Daffy—that was the gist of it—as the only other available apartment, originally promised to Marjorie, had been secured by Mr. Pope for what he called his "matutinal ablutions, videlicet tub."

"Then, when your Aunt Plessington comes, you won't have to move," said Mrs. Pope with an air of a special concession. "Your father's looking forward to seeing you, but he mustn't be disturbed just yet. He's in the vicar's study. He's had his tea in there. He's writing a letter to the Times answering something they said in a leader, and also a private note calling attention to their delay in printing his previous communication, and he wants to be delicately ironical without being in any way offensive. He wants to hint without actually threatening that very probably he will go over to the Spectator altogether if they do not become more attentive. The Times used to print his letters punctually, but latterly these automobile people seem to have got hold of it.... He has the window on the lawn open, so that I think, perhaps, we'd better not stay out here—for fear our voices might disturb him."

"Better get right round the other side of the church," said Daffy.

"He'd hear far less of us if we went indoors," said Mrs. Pope.

§ 4

The vicarage seemed tight packed with human interest for Marjorie and her mother and sisters. Going over houses is one of the amusements proper to her sex, and she and all three sisters and her mother, as soon as they had finished an inaudible tea, went to see the bedroom she was to share with Daffy, and then examined, carefully and in order, the furniture and decoration of the other bedrooms, went through the rooms downstairs, always excepting and avoiding very carefully and closing as many doors as possible on, and hushing their voices whenever they approached the study in which her father was being delicately ironical without being offensive to the Times. None of them had seen any of the vicarage people at all—Mr. Pope had come on a bicycle and managed all the negotiations—and it was curious to speculate about the individuals whose personalities pervaded the worn and faded furnishings of the place.

The Popes' keen-eyed inspection came at times, I think, dangerously near prying. The ideals of decoration and interests of the vanished family were so absolutely dissimilar to the London standards as to arouse a sort of astonished wonder in their minds. Some of the things they decided were perfectly hideous, some quaint, some were simply and weakly silly. Everything was different from Hartstone Square. Daffy was perhaps more inclined to contempt, and Mrs. Pope to refined amusement and witty appreciation than Marjorie. Marjorie felt there was something in these people that she didn't begin to understand, she needed some missing clue that would unlock the secret of their confused peculiarity. She was one of those people who have an almost instinctive turn for decoration in costume and furniture; she had already had a taste of how to do things in arranging her rooms at Bennett College, Oxbridge, where also she was in great demand among the richer girls as an adviser. She knew what it was to try and fail as well as to try and succeed, and these people, she felt, hadn't tried for anything she comprehended. She couldn't quite see why it was that there was at the same time an attempt at ornament and a disregard of beauty, she couldn't quite do as her mother did and dismiss it as an absurdity and have done with it. She couldn't understand, too, why everything should be as if it were faded and weakened from something originally bright and clear.

All the rooms were thick with queer little objects that indicated a quite beaver-like industry in the production of "work." There were embroidered covers for nearly every article on the wash-hand-stand, and mats of wool and crochet wherever anything stood on anything; there were "tidies" everywhere, and odd little brackets covered with gilded and varnished fir cones and bearing framed photographs and little jars and all sorts of colourless, dusty little objects, and everywhere on the walls tacks sustained crossed fans with badly painted flowers or transfer pictures. There was a jar on the bedroom mantel covered with varnished postage stamps and containing grey-haired dried grasses. There seemed to be a moral element in all this, for in the room Sydney shared with Rom there was a decorative piece of lettering which declared that—

There were a great number of texts that set Marjorie's mind stirring dimly with intimations of a missed significance. Over her own bed, within the lattice of an Oxford frame, was the photograph of a picture of an extremely composed young woman in a trailing robe, clinging to the Rock of Ages in the midst of histrionically aggressive waves, and she had a feeling, rather than a thought, that perhaps for all the oddity of the presentation it did convey something acutely desirable, that she herself had had moods when she would have found something very comforting in just such an impassioned grip. And on a framed, floriferous card, these incomprehensible words:

Thy Grace is Sufficient for Me.

seemed to be saying something to her tantalizingly just outside her range of apprehension.

Did all these things light up somehow to those dispossessed people—from some angle she didn't attain? Were they living and moving realities when those others were at home again?

The drawing-room had no texts; it was altogether more pretentious and less haunted by the faint and faded flavour of religion that pervaded the bedrooms. It had, however, evidences of travel in Switzerland and the Mediterranean. There was a piano in black and gold, a little out of tune, and surmounted by a Benares brass jar, enveloping a scarlet geranium in a pot. There was a Japanese screen of gold wrought upon black, that screened nothing. There was a framed chromo-lithograph of Jerusalem hot in the sunset, and another of Jerusalem cold under a sub-tropical moon, and there were gourds, roses of Jericho, sandalwood rosaries and kindred trash from the Holy Land in no little profusion upon a what-not. Such books as the room had contained had been arranged as symmetrically as possible about a large, pink-shaded lamp upon the claret-coloured cloth of a round table, and were to be replaced, Mrs. Pope said, at their departure. At present they were piled on a side-table. The girls had been through them all, and were ready with the choicer morsels for Marjorie's amusement. There was "Black Beauty," the sympathetic story of a soundly Anglican horse, and a large Bible extra-illustrated with photographs of every well-known scriptural picture from Michael Angelo to Doré, and a book of injunctions to young ladies upon their behaviour and deportment that Rom and Sydney found particularly entertaining. Marjorie discovered that Sydney had picked up a new favourite phrase. "I'm afraid we're all dreadfully cynical," said Sydney, several times.

A more advanced note was struck by a copy of "Aurora Leigh," richly underlined in pencil, but with exclamation marks at some of the bolder passages....

And presently, still avoiding the open study window very elaborately, this little group of twentieth century people went again into the church—the church whose foundations were laid in A.D. 912—foundations of rubble and cement that included flat Roman bricks from a still remoter basilica. Their voices dropped instinctively, as they came into its shaded quiet from the exterior sunshine. Marjorie went a little apart and sat in a pew that gave her a glimpse of the one good stained-glass window. Rom followed her, and perceiving her mood to be restful, sat a yard away. Syd began a whispered dispute with her mother whether it wasn't possible to try the organ, and whether Theodore might not be bribed to blow. Daffy discovered relics of a lepers' squint and a holy-water stoup, and then went to scrutinize the lettering of the ten commandments of the Mosaic law that shone black and red on gold on either side of the I.H.S. monogram behind the white-clothed communion table that had once been the altar. Upon a notice board hung about the waist of the portly pulpit were the numbers of hymns that had been sung three days ago. The sound Protestantism of the vicar had banished superfluous crosses from the building; the Bible reposed upon the wings of a great brass eagle; shining blue and crimson in the window, Saint Christopher carried his Lord. What a harmonized synthesis of conflicts a country church presents! What invisible mysteries of filiation spread between these ancient ornaments and symbols and the new young minds from the whirlpool of the town that looked upon them now with such bright, keen eyes, wondering a little, feeling a little, missing so much?

It was all so very cool and quiet now—with something of the immobile serenity of death.

§ 5

When Mr. Pope had finished his letter to the Times, he got out of the window of the study, treading on a flower-bed as he did so—he was the sort of man who treads on flower-beds—partly with the purpose of reading his composition aloud to as many members of his family as he could assemble for the purpose, and so giving them a chance of appreciating the nuances of his irony more fully than if they saw it just in cold print without the advantage of his intonation, and partly with the belated idea of welcoming Marjorie. The law presented a rather discouraging desolation. Then he became aware that the church tower frothed with his daughters. In view of his need of an audience, he decided after a brief doubt that their presence there was unobjectionable, and waved his MS. amiably. Marjorie flapped a handkerchief in reply....

The subsequent hour was just the sort of hour that gave Mr. Pope an almost meteorological importance to his family. He began with an amiability that had no fault, except, perhaps, that it was a little forced after the epistolary strain in the study, and his welcome to Marjorie was more than cordial. "Well, little Madge-cat!" he said, giving her an affectionate but sound and heavy thump on the left shoulder-blade, "got a kiss for the old daddy?"

Marjorie submitted a cheek.

"That's right," said Mr. Pope; "and now I just want you all to advise me——"

He led the way to a group of wicker garden chairs. "You're coming, mummy?" he said, and seated himself comfortably and drew out a spectacle case, while his family grouped itself dutifully. It made a charming little picture of a Man and his Womankind. "I don't often flatter myself," he said, "but this time I think I've been neat—neat's the word for it."

He cleared his throat, put on his spectacles, and emitted a long, flat preliminary note, rather like the sound of a child's trumpet. "Er—'Dear Sir!'"

"Rom," said Mrs. Pope, "don't creak your chair."

"It's Daffy, mother," said Rom.

"Oh, Rom!" said Daffy.

Mr. Pope paused, and looked with a warning eye over his left spectacle-glass at Rom.

"Don't creak your chair, Rom," he said, "when your mother tells you."

"I was not creaking my chair," said Rom.

"I heard it," said Mr. Pope, suavely.

"It was Daffy."

"Your mother does not think so," said Mr. Pope.

"Oh, all right! I'll sit on the ground," said Rom, crimson to the roots of her hair.

"Me too," said Daffy. "I'd rather."

Mr. Pope watched the transfer gravely. Then he readjusted his glasses, cleared his throat again, trumpeted, and began. "Er—'Dear Sir,'"

"Oughtn't it to be simply 'Sir,' father, for an editor?" said Marjorie.

"Perhaps I didn't explain, Marjorie," said her father, with the calm of great self-restraint, and dabbing his left hand on the manuscript in his right, "that this is a private letter—a private letter."

"I didn't understand," said Marjorie.

"It would have been evident as I went on," said Mr. Pope, and prepared to read again.

This time he was allowed to proceed, but the interruptions had ruffled him, and the gentle stresses that should have lifted the subtleties of his irony into prominence missed the words, and he had to go back and do his sentences again. Then Rom suddenly, horribly, uncontrollably, was seized with hiccups. At the second hiccup Mr. Pope paused, and looked very hard at his daughter with magnified eyes; as he was about to resume, the third burst its way through the unhappy child's utmost effort.

Mr. Pope rose with an awful resignation. "That's enough," he said. He regarded the pseudo-twin vindictively. "You haven't the self-control of a child of six," he said. Then very touchingly to Mrs. Pope: "Mummy, shall we try a game of tennis with the New Generation?"

"Can't you read it after supper?" asked Mrs. Pope.

"It must go by the eight o'clock post," said Mr. Pope, putting the masterpiece into his breast pocket, the little masterpiece that would now perhaps never be read aloud to any human being. "Daffy, dear, do you mind going in for the racquets and balls?"

The social atmosphere was now sultry, and overcast, and Mr. Pope's decision to spend the interval before Daffy returned in seeing whether he couldn't do something to the net, which was certainly very unsatisfactory, did not improve matters. Then, unhappily, Marjorie, who had got rather keen upon tennis at the Carmels', claimed her father's first two services as faults, contrary to the etiquette of the family. It happened that Mr. Pope had a really very good, hard, difficult, smart-looking serve, whose only defect was that it always went either too far or else into the net, and so a feeling had been fostered and established by his wife that, on the whole, it was advisable to regard the former variety as a legitimate extension of a father's authority. Naturally, therefore, Mr. Pope was nettled at Marjorie's ruling, and his irritation increased when his next two services to Daffy perished in the net. ("Damn that net! Puts one's eye out.") Then Marjorie gave him an unexpected soft return which he somehow muffed, and then Daffy just dropped a return over the top of the net. (Love-game.) It was then Marjorie's turn to serve, which she did with a new twist acquired from the eldest Carmel boy that struck Mr. Pope as un-English. "Go on," he said concisely. "Fifteen love."

She was gentle with her mother and they got their first rally, and when it was over Mr. Pope had to explain to Marjorie that if she returned right up into his corner of the court he would have to run backwards very fast and might fall over down the silly slope at that end. She would have to consider him and the court. One didn't get everything out of a game by playing merely to win. She said "All right, Daddy," rather off-handedly, and immediately served to him again, and he, taken a little unawares, hit the ball with the edge of his racquet and sent it out, and then he changed racquets with Daffy—it seemed he had known all along she had taken his, but he had preferred to say nothing—uttered a word of advice to his wife just on her stroke, and she, failing to grasp his intention as quickly as she ought to have done, left the score forty-fifteen. He felt better when he returned Marjorie's serve, and then before she could control herself she repeated her new unpleasant trick of playing into the corner again, whereupon, leaping back with an agility that would have shamed many a younger man, Mr. Pope came upon disaster. He went spinning down the treacherous slope behind, twisted his ankle painfully and collapsed against the iron railings of the shrubbery. It was too much, and he lost control of himself. His daughters had one instant's glimpse of the linguistic possibilities of a strong man's agony. "I told her," he went on as if he had said nothing. "Tennis!"

For a second perhaps he seemed to hesitate upon a course of action. Then as if by a great effort he took his coat from the net post and addressed himself houseward, incarnate Grand Dudgeon—limping.

"Had enough of it, Mummy," he said, and added some happily inaudible comment on Marjorie's new style of play.

The evening's exercise was at an end.

The three ladies regarded one another in silence for some moments.

"I will take in the racquets, dear," said Mrs. Pope.

"I think the other ball is at your end," said Daffy....

The apparatus put away, Marjorie and her sister strolled thoughtfully away from the house.

"There's croquet here too," said Daffy. "We've not had the things out yet!"....

"He'll play, I suppose."

"He wants to play."...

"Of course," said Marjorie after a long pause, "there's no reasoning with Dad!"

§ 6

Character is one of England's noblest and most deliberate products, but some Englishmen have it to excess. Mr. Pope had.

He was one of that large and representative class which imparts a dignity to national commerce by inheriting big businesses from its ancestors. He was a coach-builder by birth, and a gentleman by education and training. He had been to City Merchant's and Cambridge.

Throughout the earlier half of the nineteenth century the Popes had been the princes of the coach-building world. Mr. Pope's great-grandfather had been a North London wheelwright of conspicuous dexterity and integrity, who had founded the family business; his son, Mr. Pope's grandfather, had made that business the occupation of his life and brought it to the pinnacle of pre-eminence; his son, who was Marjorie's grandfather, had displayed a lesser enthusiasm, left the house at the works for a home ten miles away and sent a second son into the Church. It was in the days of the third Pope that the business ceased to expand, and began to suffer severely from the competition of an enterprising person who had originally supplied the firm with varnish, gradually picked up the trade in most other materials and accessories needed in coach-building, and passed on by almost imperceptible stages to delivering the article complete—dispensing at last altogether with the intervention of Pope and Son—to the customer. Marjorie's father had succeeded in the fulness of time to the inheritance this insurgent had damaged.

Mr. Pope was a man of firm and resentful temper, with an admiration for Cato, Brutus, Cincinnatus, Cromwell, Washington, and the sterner heroes generally, and by nature a little ill-used and offended at things. He suffered from indigestion and extreme irritability. He found himself in control of a business where more flexible virtues were needed. The Popes based their fame on a heavy, proud type of vehicle, which the increasing luxury and triviality of the age tended to replace by lighter forms of carriage, carriages with diminutive and apologetic names. As these lighter forms were not only lighter but less expensive, Mr. Pope with a pathetic confidence in the loyalty of the better class of West End customer, determined to "make a stand" against them. He was the sort of man to whom making a stand is in itself a sombre joy. If he had had to choose his pose for a portrait, he would certainly have decided to have one foot advanced, the other planted like a British oak behind, the arms folded and the brows corrugated,—making a stand.

Unhappily the stars in their courses and the general improvement of roads throughout the country fought against him. The lighter carriages, and especially the lighter carriages of that varnish-selling firm, which was now absorbing businesses right and left, prevailed over Mr. Pope's resistance. For crossing a mountain pass or fording a river, for driving over the scene of a recent earthquake or following a retreating army, for being run away with by frantic horses or crushing a personal enemy, there can be no doubt the Pope carriages remained to the very last the best possible ones and fully worth the inflexible price demanded. Unhappily all carriages in a civilization essentially decadent are not subjected to these tests, and the manufactures of his rivals were not only much cheaper, but had a sort of meretricious smartness, a disingenuous elasticity, above all a levity, hateful indeed to the spirit of Mr. Pope yet attractive to the wanton customer. Business dwindled. Nevertheless the habitual element in the good class customer did keep things going, albeit on a shrinking scale, until Mr. Pope came to the unfortunate decision that he would make a stand against automobiles. He regarded them as an intrusive nuisance which had to be seen only to be disowned by the landed gentry of England. Rather than build a car he said he would go out of business. He went out of business. Within five years of this determination he sold out the name, good will, and other vestiges of his concern to a mysterious buyer who turned out to be no more than an agent for these persistently expanding varnish makers, and he retired with a genuine grievance upon the family accumulations—chiefly in Consols and Home Railways.

He refused however to regard his defeat as final, put great faith in the approaching exhaustion of the petrol supply, and talked in a manner that should have made the Automobile Association uneasy, of devoting the rest of his days to the purification of England from these aggressive mechanisms. "It was a mistake," he said, "to let them in." He became more frequent at his excellent West End club, and directed a certain portion of his capital to largely indecisive but on the whole unprofitable speculations in South African and South American enterprises. He mingled a little in affairs. He was a tough conventional speaker, rich in established phrases and never abashed by hearing himself say commonplace things, and in addition to his campaign against automobiles he found time to engage also in quasi-political activities, taking chairs, saying a few words and so on, cherishing a fluctuating hope that his eloquence might ultimately win him an invitation to contest a constituency in the interests of reaction and the sounder elements in the Liberal party.

He had a public-spirited side, and he was particularly attracted by that mass of modern legislative proposals which aims at a more systematic control of the lives of lower class persons for their own good by their betters. Indeed, in the first enthusiasm of his proprietorship of the Pope works at East Purblow, he had organized one of those benevolent industrial experiments that are now so common. He felt strongly against the drink evil, that is to say, the unrestricted liberty of common people to drink what they prefer, and he was acutely impressed by the fact that working-class families do not spend their money in the way that seems most desirable to upper middle-class critics. Accordingly he did his best to replace the dangerous freedoms of money by that ideal of the social reformer, Payment in Kind. To use his invariable phrase, the East Purblow experiment did "no mean service" to the cause of social reform. Unhappily it came to an end through a prosecution under the Truck Act, that blot upon the Statute Book, designed, it would appear, even deliberately to vitiate man's benevolent control of his fellow man. The lessons to be drawn from that experience, however, grew if anything with the years. He rarely spoke without an allusion to it, and it was quite remarkable how readily it could be adapted to illuminate a hundred different issues in the hospitable columns of the Spectator....

§ 7

At seven o'clock Marjorie found herself upstairs changing into her apple-green frock. She had had a good refreshing wash in cold soft water, and it was pleasant to change into thinner silk stockings and dainty satin slippers and let down and at last brush her hair and dress loiteringly after the fatigues of her journey and the activities of her arrival. She looked out on the big church and the big trees behind it against the golden quiet of a summer evening with extreme approval.

"I suppose those birds are rooks," she said.

But Daffy had gone to see that the pseudo-twins had done themselves justice in their muslin frocks and pink sashes; they were apt to be a little sketchy with their less accessible buttons.

Marjorie became aware of two gentlemen with her mother on the lawn below.

One was her almost affianced lover, Will Magnet, the humorous writer. She had been doing her best not to think about him all day, but now he became an unavoidable central fact. She regarded him with an almost perplexed scrutiny, and wondered vividly why she had been so excited and pleased by his attentions during the previous summer.

Mr. Magnet was one of those quiet, deliberately unassuming people who do not even attempt to be beautiful. Not for him was it to pretend, but to prick the bladder of pretence. He was a fairish man of forty, pale, with a large protuberant, observant grey eye—I speak particularly of the left—and a face of quiet animation warily alert for the wit's opportunity. His nose and chin were pointed, and his lips thin and quaintly pressed together. He was dressed in grey, with a low-collared silken shirt showing a thin neck, and a flowing black tie, and he carried a grey felt hat in his joined hands behind his back. She could hear the insinuating cadences of his voice as he talked in her mother's ear. The other gentleman, silent on her mother's right, must, she knew, be Mr. Wintersloan, whom Mr. Magnet had proposed to bring over. His dress betrayed that modest gaiety of disposition becoming in an artist, and indeed he was one of Mr. Magnet's favourite illustrators. He was in a dark bluish-grey suit; a black tie that was quite unusually broad went twice around his neck before succumbing to the bow, and his waistcoat appeared to be of some gaily-patterned orange silk. Marjorie's eyes returned to Mr. Magnet. Hitherto she had never had an opportunity of remarking that his hair was more than a little attenuated towards the crown. It was funny how his tie came out under his chin to the right.

What an odd thing men's dress had become, she thought. Why did they wear those ridiculous collars and ties? Why didn't they always dress in flannels and look as fine and slender and active as the elder Carmel boy for example? Mr. Magnet couldn't be such an ill-shaped man. Why didn't every one dress to be just as beautiful and splendid as possible?—instead of wearing queer things!

"Coming down?" said Daffy, a vision of sulphur-yellow, appearing in the doorway.

"Let them go first," said Marjorie, with a finer sense of effect. "And Theodore. We don't want to make part of a comic entry with Theodore, Daffy."

Accordingly, the two sisters watched discreetly—they had to be wary on account of Mr. Magnet's increasingly frequent glances at the windows—and when at last all the rest of the family had appeared below, they decided their cue had come. Mr. Pope strolled into the group, with no trace of his recent debacle except a slight limp. He was wearing a jacket of damson-coloured velvet, which he affected in the country, and all traces of his Grand Dudgeon were gone. But then he rarely had Grand Dudgeon except in the sanctities of family life, and hardly ever when any other man was about.

"Well," his daughters heard him say, with a witty allusiveness that was difficult to follow, "so the Magnet has come to the Mountain again—eh?"

"Come on, Madge," said Daffy, and the two sisters emerged harmoniously together from the house.

It would have been manifest to a meaner capacity than any present that evening that Mr. Magnet regarded Marjorie with a distinguished significance. He had two eyes, but he had that mysterious quality so frequently associated with a bluish-grey iris which gives the effect of looking hard with one large orb, a sort of grey searchlight effect, and he used this eye ray now to convey a respectful but firm admiration in the most unequivocal manner. He saluted Daffy courteously, and then allowed himself to retain Marjorie's hand for just a second longer than was necessary as he said—very simply—

"I am very pleased indeed to meet you again—very."

A slight embarrassment fell between them.

"You are staying near here, Mr. Magnet?"

"At the inn," said Mr. Magnet, and then, "I chose it because it would be near you."

His eye pressed upon her again for a moment.

"Is it comfortable?" said Marjorie.

"So charmingly simple," said Mr. Magnet. "I love it."

A tinkling bell announced the preparedness of supper, and roused the others to th consciousness that they were silently watching Mr. Magnet and Marjorie.

"It's quite a simple farmhouse supper," said Mrs. Pope.

§ 8

There were ducks, green peas, and adolescent new potatoes for supper, and afterwards stewed fruit and cream and junket and cheese, bottled beer, Gilbey's Burgundy, and home-made lemonade. Mrs. Pope carved, because Mr. Pope splashed too much, and bones upset him and made him want to show up chicken in the Times. So he sat at the other end and rallied his guests while Mrs. Pope distributed the viands. He showed not a trace of his recent umbrage. Theodore sat between Daffy and his mother because of his table manners, and Marjorie was on her father's right hand and next to Mr. Wintersloan, while Mr. Magnet was in the middle of the table on the opposite side in a position convenient for looking at her. Both maids waited.

The presence of Magnet invariably stirred the latent humorist in Mr. Pope. He felt that he who talks to humorists should himself be humorous, and it was his private persuasion that with more attention he might have been, to use a favourite form of expression, "no mean jester." Quite a lot of little things of his were cherished as "Good" both by himself and, with occasional inaccuracies, by Mrs. Pope. He opened out now in a strain of rich allusiveness.

"What will you drink, Mr. Wintersloan?" he said. "Wine of the country, yclept beer, red wine from France, or my wife's potent brew from the golden lemon?"

Mr. Wintersloan thought he would take Burgundy. Mr. Magnet preferred beer.

> "I've heard there's iron in the Beer,
> And I believe it,"

misquoted Mr. Pope, and nodded as it were to the marker to score. "Daffy and Marjorie are still in the lemonade stage. Will you take a little Burgundy to-night, Mummy?"

Mrs. Pope decided she would, and was inspired to ask Mr. Wintersloan if he had been in that part of the country before. Topography ensued. Mr. Wintersloan had a style of his own, and spoke of the Buryhamstreet district as a "pooty little country—pooty little hills, with a swirl in them."

This pleased Daffy and Marjorie, and their eyes met for a moment.

Then Mr. Magnet, with a ray full on Marjorie, said he had always been fond of Surrey. "I think if ever I made a home in the country I should like it to be here."

Mr. Wintersloan said Surrey would tire him, it was too bossy and curly, too flocculent; he would prefer to look on broader, simpler lines, with just a sudden catch in the breath in them—if you understand me?

Marjorie did, and said so.

"A sob—such as you get at the break of a pinewood on a hill."

This baffled Mr. Pope, but Marjorie took it. "Or the short dry cough of a cliff," she said.

"Exactly," said Mr. Wintersloan, and having turned a little deliberate close-lipped smile on her for a moment, resumed his wing.

"So long as a landscape doesn't sneeze" said Mr. Magnet, in that irresistible dry way of his, and Rom and Sydney, at any rate, choked.

"Now is the hour when Landscapes yawn," mused Mr. Pope, coming in all right at the end.

Then Mrs. Pope asked Mr. Wintersloan, about his route to Buryhamstreet, and then Mr. Pope asked Mr. Magnet whether he was playing at a new work or working at a new play.

Mr. Magnet said he was dreaming over a play. He wanted to bring out the more serious side of his humour, go a little deeper into things than he had hitherto done.

"Mingling smiles and tears," said Mr. Pope approvingly.

Mr. Magnet said very quietly that all true humour did that.

Then Mrs. Pope asked what the play was to be about, and Mr. Magnet, who seemed disinclined to give an answer, turned the subject by saying he had to prepare an address on humour for the next dinner of the Literati. "It's to be a humourist's dinner, and they've made me the guest of the evening—by way of a joke to begin with," he said with that dry smile again.

Mrs. Pope said he shouldn't say things like that. She then said "Syd!" quietly but sharply to Sydney, who was making a disdainful, squinting face at Theodore, and told the parlourmaid to clear the plates for sweets. Mr. Magnet professed great horror of public speaking. He said that whenever he rose to make an after-dinner speech all the ices he had ever eaten seemed to come out of the past, and sit on his backbone.

The talk centered for awhile on Mr. Magnet's address, and apropos of Tests of Humour Mr. Pope, who in his way was "no mean raconteur," related the story of the man who took the salad dressing with his hand, and when his host asked why he did that, replied: "Oh! I thought it was spinach!"

"Many people," added Mr. Pope, "wouldn't see the point of that. And if they don't see the point they can't—and the more they try the less they do."

All four girls hoped secretly and not too confidently that their laughter had not sounded hollow.

And then for a time the men told stories as they came into their heads in an easy, irresponsible way. Mr. Magnet spoke of the humour of the omnibus-driver who always dangled and twiddled his badge "by way of a joke" when he passed the conductor whose father had been hanged, and Mr. Pope, perhaps, a little irrelevantly, told the story of the little boy who was asked his father's last words, and said "mother was with him to the end," which particularly amused Mrs. Pope. Mr. Wintersloan gave the story of the woman who was taking her son to the hospital with his head jammed into a saucepan, and explained to the other people in the omnibus: "You see, what makes it so annoying, it's me only saucepan!" Then they came back to the Sense of Humour with the dentist who shouted with laughter, and when asked the reason by his patient, choked out: "Wrong tooth!" and then Mr. Pope reminded them of the heartless husband who, suddenly informed that his mother-in-law was dead, exclaimed "Oh, don't make me laugh, please, I've got a split lip...."

§ 9

The conversation assumed a less anecdotal quality with the removal to the drawing-room. On Mr. Magnet's initiative the gentlemen followed the ladies almost immediately, and it was Mr. Magnet who remembered that Marjorie could sing.

Both the elder sisters indeed had sweet clear voices, and they had learnt a number of those jolly songs the English made before the dull Hanoverians came. Syd accompanied, and Rom sat back in the low chair in the corner and fell deeply in love with Mr. Wintersloan. The three musicians in their green and sulphur-yellow and white made a pretty group in the light of the shaded lamp against the black and gold Broadwood, the tawdry screen, its pattern thin glittering upon darkness, and the deep shadows behind. Marjorie loved singing, and forgot herself as she sang.

> "I love, and he loves me again,
> Yet dare I not tell who;
> For if the nymphs should know my swain,
> I fear they'd love him too,"

she sang, and Mr. Magnet could not conceal the intensity of his admiration.

Mr. Pope had fallen into a pleasant musing; several other ripe old yarns, dear delicious old things, had come into his mind that he felt he might presently recall when this unavoidable display of accomplishments was overpast, and it was with one of them almost on his lips that he glanced across at his guest.

He was surprised to see Mr. Magnet's face transfigured. He was sitting forward, looking up at Marjorie, and he had caught something of the expression of those blessed boys who froth at the feet of an Assumption. For an instant Mr. Pope did not understand.

Then he understood. It was Marjorie! He had a twinge of surprise, and glanced at his own daughter as though he had never seen her before. He perceived in a flash for the first time that this troublesome, clever, disrespectful child was tall and shapely and sweet, and indeed quite a beautiful young woman. He forgot his anecdotes. His being was suffused with pride and responsibility and the sense of virtue rewarded. He did not reflect for a moment that Marjorie embodied in almost equal proportions the very best points in his mother and his mother-in-law, and avoided his own more salient characteristics with so neat a dexterity that from top to toe, except for the one matter of colour, not only did she not resemble him but she scarcely even alluded to him. He thought simply that she was his daughter, that she derived from him, that her beauty was his. She was the outcome of his meritorious preparations. He recalled all the moments when he had been kind and indulgent to her, all the bills he had paid for her; all the stresses and trials of the coach-building collapse, all the fluctuations of his speculative adventures, became things he had faced patiently and valiantly for her sake. He forgot the endless times when he had been viciously cross with her, all the times when he had pished and tushed and sworn in her hearing. He had on provocation and in spite of her mother's protests slapped her pretty vigorously, but such things are better forgotten; nor did he recall how bitterly he had opposed the college education which had made her now so clear in eye and thought, nor the frightful shindy, only three months since, about that identical green dress in which she now stood delightful. He forgot these petty details, as an idealist should. There she was, his daughter. An immense benevolence irradiated his soul—for Marjorie—for Magnet. His eyes were suffused with a not ignoble tenderness. The man, he knew, was worth at least thirty-five thousand pounds, a discussion of investments had made that clear, and he must be making at least five thousand a year! A beautiful girl, a worthy man! A good fellow, a sound good fellow, a careful fellow too—as these fellows went!

Old Daddy would lose his treasure of course.

Well, a father must learn resignation, and he for one would not stand in the way of his girl's happiness. A day would come when, very beautifully and tenderly, he would hand her over to Magnet, his favourite daughter to his trusted friend. "Well, my boy, there's no one in all the world——" he would begin.

It would be a touching parting. "Don't forget your old father, Maggots," he would say. At such a moment that quaint nickname would surely not be resented....

He reflected how much he had always preferred Marjorie to Daffy. She was brighter—more like him. Daffy was unresponsive, with a touch of bitterness under her tongue....

He was already dreaming he was a widower, rather infirm, the object of Magnet's and Marjorie's devoted care, when the song ceased, and the wife he had for the purpose of reveries just consigned so carelessly to the cemetery proposed that they should have a little game that every one could play at. A number of pencils and slips of paper appeared in her hands.

She did not want the girls to exhaust their repertory on this first occasion—and besides, Mr. Pope liked games in which one did things with pencils and strips of paper. Mr. Magnet wished the singing to go on, he said, but he was overruled.

So for a time every one played a little game in which Mr. Pope was particularly proficient. Indeed, it was rare that any one won but Mr. Pope. It was called "The Great Departed," and it had such considerable educational value that all the children had to play at it whenever he wished.

It was played in this manner; one of the pseudo twins opened a book and dabbed a finger on the page, and read out the letter immediately at the tip of her finger, then all of them began to write as hard as they could, writing down the names of every great person they could think of, whose name began with that letter. At the end of five minutes Mr. Pope said Stop! and then began to read his list out, beginning with the first name. Everybody who had that name crossed it out and scored one, and after his list was exhausted all the surviving names on the next list were read over in the same way, and so on. The names had to be the names of dead celebrated people, only one monarch of the same name of the same dynasty was allowed, and Mr. Pope adjudicated on all doubtful cases. It was great fun.

The first two games were won as usual by Mr. Pope, and then Mr. Wintersloan, who had been a little distraught in his manner, brightened up and scribbled furiously.

The letter was D, and after Mr. Pope had rehearsed a tale of nine and twenty names, Mr. Wintersloan read out his list in that curious voice of his which suggested nothing so much as some mobile drink glucking out of the neck of a bottle held upside down.

"Dahl," he began.

"Who was Dahl?" asked Mr. Pope.

"'Vented dahlias," said Mr. Wintersloan, with a sigh. "Danton."

"Forgot him," said Mr. Pope.

"Davis."

"Davis?"

"Davis Straits. Doe."

"Who?"

"John Doe, Richard Roe."

"Legal fiction, I'm afraid," said Mr. Pope.

"Dam," said Mr. Wintersloan, and added after a slight pause: "Anthony van."

Mr. Pope made an interrogative noise.

"Painter—eighteenth century—Dutch. Dam, Jan van, his son. Dam, Frederich van. Dam, Wilhelm van. Dam, Diedrich van. Dam, Wilhelmina, wood engraver, gifted woman. Diehl."

"Who?"

"Painter—dead—famous. See Düsseldorf. It's all painters now—all guaranteed dead, all good men. Deeds of Norfolk, the aquarellist, Denton, Dibbs."

"Er?" said Mr. Pope.

"The Warwick Claude, you know. Died 1823."

"Dickson, Dunting, John Dickery. Peter Dickery, William Dock—I beg your pardon?"

Mr. Pope was making a protesting gesture, but Mr. Wintersloan's bearing was invincible, and he proceeded.

In the end he emerged triumphant with forty-nine names, mostly painters for whose fame he answered, but whose reputations were certainly new to every one else present. "I can go on like that," said Mr. Wintersloan, "with any letter," and turned that hard little smile full on Marjorie. "I didn't see how to do it at first. I just cast about.

But I know a frightful lot of painters. No end. Shall we try again?"

Marjorie glanced at her father. Mr. Wintersloan's methods were all too evident to her. A curious feeling pervaded the room that Mr. Pope didn't think Mr. Wintersloan's conduct honourable, and that he might even go some way towards saying so.

So Mrs. Pope became very brisk and stirring, and said she thought that now perhaps a charade would be more amusing. It didn't do to keep on at a game too long. She asked Rom and Daphne and Theodore and Mr. Wintersloan to go out, and they all agreed readily, particularly Rom. "Come on!" said Rom to Mr. Wintersloan. Everybody else shifted into an audience-like group between the piano and the what-not. Mr. Magnet sat at Marjorie's feet, while Syd played a kind of voluntary, and Mr. Pope leant back in his chair, with his brows knit and lips moving, trying to remember something.

The charade was very amusing. The word was Catarrh, and Mr. Wintersloan, as the patient in the last act being given gruel, surpassed even the children's very high expectations. Rom, as his nurse, couldn't keep her hands off him. Then the younger people kissed round and were packed off to bed, and the rest of the party went to the door upon the lawn and admired the night. It was a glorious summer night, deep blue, and rimmed warmly by the afterglow, moonless, and with a few big lamp-like stars above the black still shapes of trees.

Mrs. Pope said they would all accompany their guests to the gate at the end of the avenue—in spite of the cockchafers.

Mr. Pope's ankle, however, excused him; the cordiality of his parting from Mr. Wintersloan seemed a trifle forced, and he limped thoughtfully and a little sombrely towards the study to see if he could find an Encyclopædia or some such book of reference that would give the names of the lesser lights of Dutch, Italian, and English painting during the last two centuries.

He felt that Mr. Wintersloan had established an extraordinarily bad precedent.

§ 10

Marjorie discovered that she and Mr. Magnet had fallen a little behind the others. She would have quickened her pace, but Mr. Magnet stopped short and said: "Marjorie!"

"When I saw you standing there and singing," said Mr. Magnet, and was short of breath for a moment.

Marjorie's natural gift for interruption failed her altogether.

"I felt I would rather be able to call you mine—than win an empire."

The pause seemed to lengthen, between them, and Marjorie's remark when she made it at last struck her even as she made it as being but poorly conceived. She had some weak idea of being self-depreciatory.

"I think you had better win an empire, Mr. Magnet," she said meekly.

Then, before anything more was possible, they had come up to Daffy and Mr. Wintersloan and her mother at the gate....

As they returned Mrs. Pope was loud in the praises of Will Magnet. She had a little clear-cut voice, very carefully and very skilfully controlled, and she dilated on his modesty, his quiet helpfulness at table, his ready presence of mind. She pointed out instances of those admirable traits, incidents small in themselves but charming in their implications. When somebody wanted junket, he had made no fuss, he had just helped them to junket. "So modest and unassuming," sang Mrs. Pope. "You'd never dream he was quite rich and famous. Yet every book he writes is translated into Russian and German and all sorts of languages. I suppose he's almost the greatest humorist we have. That play of his; what is it called?—Our Owd Woman—has been performed nearly twelve hundred times! I think that is the most wonderful of gifts. Think of the people it has made happy."

The conversation was mainly monologue. Both Marjorie and Daffy were unusually thoughtful.

§ 11

Marjorie ended the long day in a worldly mood.

"Penny for your thoughts," said Daffy abruptly, brushing the long firelit rapids of her hair.

"Not for sale," said Marjorie, and roused herself. "I've had a long day."

"It's always just the time I particularly wish I was a man," she remarked after a brief return to meditation. "Fancy, no hair-pins, no brushing, no tie-up to get lost about, no strings. I suppose they haven't strings?"

"They haven't," said Daffy with conviction.

She met Marjorie's interrogative eye. "Father would swear at them," she explained. "He'd naturally tie himself up—and we should hear of it."

"I didn't think of that," said Marjorie, and stuck out her chin upon her fists. "Sound induction."

She forgot this transitory curiosity.

"Suppose one had a maid, Daffy—a real maid ... a maid who mended your things ... did your hair while you read...."

"Oh! here goes," and she stood up and grappled with the task of undressing.

CHAPTER THE SECOND

The Two Proposals of Mr. Magnet

§ 1

It was presently quite evident to Marjorie that Mr. Magnet intended to propose marriage to her, and she did not even know whether she wanted him to do so.

She had met him first the previous summer while she had been staying with the Petley-Cresthams at High Windower, and it had been evident that he found her extremely attractive. She had never had a real grown man at her feet before, and she had found it amazingly entertaining. She had gone for a walk with him the morning before she came away—a frank and ingenuous proceeding that made Mrs. Petley-Crestham say the girl knew what she was about, and she had certainly coquetted with him in an extraordinary manner at golf-croquet. After that Oxbridge had swallowed her up, and though he had called once on her mother while Marjorie was in London during the Christmas vacation, he hadn't seen her again. He had written—which was exciting—a long friendly humorous letter about nothing in particular, with an air of its being quite the correct thing for him to do, and she had answered, and there had been other exchanges. But all sorts of things had happened in the interval, and Marjorie had let him get into quite a back place in her thoughts—the fact that he was a member of her father's club had seemed somehow to remove him from a great range of possibilities—until a drift in her mother's talk towards him and a letter from him with an indefinable change in tone towards intimacy, had restored him to importance.

Now here he was in the foreground of her world again, evidently more ardent than ever, and with a portentous air of being about to do something decisive at the very first opportunity. What was he going to do? What had her mother been hinting at? And what, in fact, did the whole thing amount to?

Marjorie was beginning to realize that this was going to be a very serious affair indeed for her—and that she was totally unprepared to meet it.

It had been very amusing, very amusing indeed, at the Petley-Cresthams', but there were moments now when she felt towards Mr. Magnet exactly as she would have felt if he had been one of the Oxbridge tradesmen hovering about her with a "little account," full of apparently exaggerated items....

Her thoughts and feelings were all in confusion about this business. Her mind was full of scraps, every sort of idea, every sort of attitude contributed something to that Twentieth Century jumble. For example, and so far as its value went among motives, it was by no means a trivial consideration; she wanted a proposal for its own sake. Daffy had had a proposal last year, and although it wasn't any sort of eligible proposal, still there it was, and she had given herself tremendous airs. But Marjorie would certainly have preferred some lighter kind of proposal than that which now threatened her. She felt that behind Mr. Magnet were sanctions; that she wasn't free to deal with this proposal as she liked. He was at Buryhamstreet almost with the air of being her parents' guest.

Less clear and more instinctive than her desire for a proposal was her inclination to see just all that Mr. Magnet was disposed to do, and hear all that he was disposed to say. She was curious. He didn't behave in the least as she had expected a lover to behave.

But then none of the boys, the "others" with whom she had at times stretched a hand towards the hem of emotion, had ever done that. She had an obscure feeling that perhaps presently Mr. Magnet must light up, be stirred and stirring. Even now his voice changed very interestingly when he was alone with her. His breath seemed to go—as though something had pricked his lung. If it hadn't been for that new, disconcerting realization of an official pressure behind him, I think she would have been quite ready to experiment extensively with his emotions....

But she perceived as she lay awake next morning that she wasn't free for experiments any longer. What she might say or do now would be taken up very conclusively. And she had no idea what she wanted to say or do.

Marriage regarded in the abstract—that is to say, with Mr. Magnet out of focus—was by no means an unattractive proposal to her. It was very much at the back of Marjorie's mind that after Oxbridge, unless she was prepared to face a very serious row indeed and go to teach in a school—and she didn't feel any call whatever to teach in a school—she would probably have to return to Hartstone Square and share Daffy's room again, and assist in the old collective, wearisome task of propitiating her father. The freedoms of Oxbridge had enlarged her imagination until that seemed an almost unendurably irksome prospect. She had tasted life as it could be in her father's absence, and she was beginning to realize just what an impossible person he was. Marriage was escape from all that; it meant not only respectful parents but a house of her very own, furniture of her choice, great freedom of movement, an authority, an importance. She had seen what it meant to be a prosperously married young woman in the person of one or two resplendent old girls revisiting Bennett College, scattering invitations, offering protections and opportunities....

Of course there is love.

Marjorie told herself, as she had been trained to tell herself, to be sensible, but something within her repeated: there is love.

Of course she liked Mr. Magnet. She really did like Mr. Magnet very much. She had had her girlish dreams, had fallen in love with pictures of men and actors and a music master and a man who used to ride by as she went to school; but wasn't this desolating desire for self-abandonment rather silly?—something that one left behind with much else when it came to putting up one's hair and sensible living, something to blush secretly about and hide from every eye?

Among other discrepant views that lived together in her mind as cats and rats and parrots and squirrels and so forth used to live together in those Happy Family cages unseemly men in less well-regulated days were wont to steer about our streets, was one instilled by quite a large proportion of the novels she had read, that a girl was a sort of self-giving prize for high moral worth. Mr. Magnet she knew was good, was kind, was brave with that truer courage, moral courage, which goes with his type of physique; he was modest, unassuming, well off and famous, and very much in love with her. His True Self, as Mrs. Pope had pointed out several times, must be really very beautiful, and in some odd way a line of Shakespeare had washed up in her consciousness as being somehow effectual on his behalf:

"Love looks not with the eye but with the mind."

She felt she ought to look with the mind. Nice people surely never looked in any other way. It seemed from this angle almost her duty to love him....

Perhaps she did love him, and mistook the symptoms. She did her best to mistake the symptoms. But if she did truly love him, would it seem so queer and important and antagonistic as it did that his hair was rather thin upon the crown of his head?

She wished she hadn't looked down on him....

Poor Marjorie! She was doing her best to be sensible, and she felt herself adrift above a clamorous abyss of feared and forbidden thoughts. Down there she knew well enough it wasn't thus that love must come. Deep in her soul, the richest thing in her life indeed and the best thing she had to give humanity, was a craving for beauty that at times became almost intolerable, a craving for something other than beauty and yet inseparably allied with it, a craving for deep excitement, for a sort of glory in adventure, for passion—for things akin to great music and heroic poems and bannered traditions of romance. She had hidden away in her an immense tumultuous appetite for life, an immense tumultuous capacity for living. To be loved beautifully was surely the crown and climax of her being.

She did not dare to listen to these deeps, yet these insurgent voices filled her. Even while she drove her little crocodile of primly sensible thoughts to their sane appointed conclusion, her blood and nerves and all her being were protesting that Mr. Magnet would not do, that whatever other worthiness was in him, regarded as a lover he was preposterous and flat and foolish and middle-aged, and that it were better never to have lived than to put the treasure of her life to his meagre lips and into his hungry, unattractive arms. "The ugliness of it! The spiritless horror of it!" so dumbly and formlessly the rebel voices urged.

"One has to be sensible," said Marjorie to herself, suddenly putting down Shaw's book on Municipal Trading, which she imagined she had been reading....

(Perhaps all marriage was horrid, and one had to get over it.)

That was rather what her mother had conveyed to her.

§ 2

Mr. Magnet made his first proposal in form three days later, after coming twice to tea and staying on to supper. He had played croquet with Mr. Pope, he had been beaten twelve times in spite of twinges in the sprained ankle—heroically borne—had had three victories lucidly explained away, and heard all the particulars of the East Purblow experiment three times over, first in relation to the new Labour Exchanges, then regarded at rather a different angle in relation to female betting, tally-men, and the sanctities of the home generally, and finally in a more exhaustive style, to show its full importance from every side and more particularly as demonstrating the gross injustice done to Mr. Pope by the neglect of its lessons, a neglect too systematic to be accidental, in the social reform literature of the time. Moreover, Mr. Magnet had been made to understand thoroughly how several later quasi-charitable attempts of a similar character had already become, or must inevitably become, unsatisfactory through their failure to follow exactly in the lines laid down by Mr. Pope.

Mr. Pope was really very anxious to be pleasant and agreeable to Mr. Magnet, and he could think of no surer way of doing so than by giving him an unrestrained intimacy of conversation that prevented anything more than momentary intercourse between his daughter and her admirer. And not only did Mr. Magnet find it difficult to get away from Mr. Pope without offence, but whenever by any chance Mr. Pope was detached for a moment Mr. Magnet discovered that Marjorie either wasn't to be seen, or if she was she wasn't to be isolated by any device he could contrive, before the unappeasable return of Mr. Pope.

Mr. Magnet did not get his chance therefore until Lady Petchworth's little gathering at Summerhay Park.

Lady Petchworth was Mrs. Pope's oldest friend, and one of those brighter influences which save our English country-side from lassitude. She had been more fortunate than Mrs. Pope, for while Mr. Pope with that aptitude for disadvantage natural to his temperament had, he said, been tied to a business that never gave him a chance, Lady Petchworth's husband had been a reckless investor of exceptional good-luck. In particular, led by a dream, he had put most of his money into a series of nitrate deposits in caves in Saghalien haunted by benevolent penguins, and had been rewarded beyond the dreams of avarice. His foresight had received the fitting reward of a knighthood, and Sir Thomas, after restoring the Parish Church at Summerhay in a costly and destructive manner, spent his declining years in an enviable contentment with Lady Petchworth and the world at large, and died long before infirmity made him really troublesome.

Good fortune had brought out Lady Petchworth's social aptitudes. Summerhay Park was everything that a clever woman, inspired by that gardening literature which has been so abundant in the opening years of the twentieth century, could make it. It had rosaries and rock gardens, sundials and yew hedges, pools and ponds, lead figures and stone urns, box borderings and wilderness corners and hundreds and hundreds of feet of prematurely-aged red-brick wall with broad herbaceous borders; the walks had primroses, primulas and cowslips in a quite disingenuous abundance, and in spring the whole extent of the park was gay, here with thousands of this sort of daffodil just bursting out and here with thousands of that sort of narcissus just past its prime, and every patch ready to pass itself off in its naturalized way as the accidental native flower of the field, if only it hadn't been for all the other different varieties coming on or wilting-off in adjacent patches....

Her garden was only the beginning of Lady Petchworth's activities. She had a model dairy, and all her poultry was white, and so far as she was able to manage it she made Summerhay a model village. She overflowed with activities, it was astonishing in one so plump and blonde, and meeting followed meeting in the artistic little red-brick and green-stained timber village hall she had erected. Now it was the National Theatre and now it was the National Mourning; now it was the Break Up of the Poor Law, and now the Majority Report, now the Mothers' Union, and now Socialism, and now Individualism, but always something progressive and beneficial. She did her best to revive the old village life, and brought her very considerable powers of compulsion to make the men dance in simple old Morris dances, dressed up in costumes they secretly abominated, and to induce the mothers to dress their children in art-coloured smocks instead of the prints and blue serge frocks they preferred. She did not despair, she said, of creating a spontaneous peasant art movement in the district, springing from the people and expressing the people, but so far it had been necessary to import not only instructors and material, but workers to keep the thing going, so sluggish had the spontaneity of our English countryside become.

Her little gatherings were quite distinctive of her. They were a sort of garden party extending from mid-day to six or seven; there would be a nucleus of house guests, and the highways and byeways on every hand would be raided to supply persons and interests. She had told her friend to "bring the girls over for the day," and flung an invitation to Mr. Pope, who had at once excused himself on the score of his ankle. Mr. Pope was one of those men who shun social gatherings—ostensibly because of a sterling simplicity of taste, but really because his intolerable egotism made him feel slighted and neglected on these occasions. He told his wife he would be far happier with a book at home, exhorted her not to be late, and was seen composing himself to read the "Vicar of Wakefield"—whenever they published a new book Mr. Pope pretended to read an old one—as the hired waggonette took the rest of his family— Theodore very unhappy in buff silk and a wide Stuart collar—down the avenue.

They found a long lunch table laid on the lawn beneath the chestnuts, and in full view of the poppies and forget-me-nots around the stone obelisk, a butler and three men servants with brass buttons and red and white striped waistcoats gave dignity to the scene, and beyond, on the terrace amidst abundance of deckchairs, cane chairs, rugs, and cushions, a miscellaneous and increasing company seethed under Lady Petchworth's plump but entertaining hand. There were, of course, Mr. Magnet, and his friend Mr. Wintersloan—Lady Petchworth had been given to understand how the land lay; and there was Mr. Bunford Paradise the musician, who was doing his best to teach a sullen holiday class in the village schoolroom to sing the artless old folk songs of Surrey again, in spite of the invincible persuasion of everybody in the class that the songs were rather indelicate and extremely silly; there were the Rev. Jopling Baynes, and two Cambridge undergraduates in flannels, and a Doctor something or other from London. There was also the Hon. Charles Muskett, Lord Pottinger's cousin and estate agent, in tweeds and very helpful. The ladies included Mrs. Raff, the well-known fashion writer, in a wonderful costume, the anonymous doctor's wife, three or four neighbouring mothers with an undistinguished daughter or so, and two quiet-mannered middle-aged ladies, whose names Marjorie could not catch, and whom Lady Petchworth, in that well-controlled voice of hers, addressed as Kate and Julia, and seemed on the whole disposed to treat as humorous. There was also Fraulein Schmidt in charge of Lady Petchworth's three tall and already abundant children, Prunella, Prudence, and Mary, and a young, newly-married couple of cousins, who addressed each other in soft undertones and sat apart. These were the chief items that became distinctive in Marjorie's survey; but there were a number of other people who seemed to come and go, split up, fuse, change their appearance slightly, and behave in the way inadequately apprehended people do behave on these occasions.

Marjorie very speedily found her disposition to take a detached and amused view of the entertainment in conflict with more urgent demands. From the outset Mr. Magnet loomed upon her—he loomed nearer and nearer. He turned his eye upon her as she came up to the wealthy expanse of Lady Petchworth's presence, like some sort of obsolescent iron-clad turning a dull-grey, respectful, loving searchlight upon a fugitive torpedo boat, and thereafter he seemed to her to be looking at her without intermission, relentlessly, and urging himself towards her. She wished he wouldn't. She hadn't at all thought he would on this occasion.

At first she relied upon her natural powers of evasion, and the presence of a large company. Then gradually it became apparent that Lady Petchworth and her mother, yes—and the party generally, and the gardens and the weather and the stars in their courses were of a mind to co-operate in giving opportunity for Mr. Magnet's unmistakable intentions.

And Marjorie with that instability of her sex which has been a theme for masculine humour in all ages, suddenly and with an extraordinary violence didn't want to make up her mind about Mr. Magnet. She didn't want to accept him; and as distinctly she didn't want to refuse him. She didn't even want to be thought about as making up her mind about him—which was, so to speak, an enlargement of her previous indisposition. She didn't even want to seem to avoid him, or to be thinking about him, or aware of his existence.

After the greeting of Lady Petchworth she had succeeded very clumsily in not seeing Mr. Magnet, and had addressed herself to Mr. Wintersloan, who was standing a little apart, looking under his hand, with one eye shut, at the view between the tree stems towards Buryhamstreet. He told her that he thought he had found something "pooty" that hadn't been done, and she did her best to share his artistic interests with a vivid sense of Mr. Magnet's tentative incessant approach behind her.

He joined them, and she made a desperate attempt to entangle Mr. Wintersloan in a three-cornered talk in vain. He turned away at the first possible opportunity, and left her to an embarrassed and eloquently silent tête-à-tête. Mr. Magnet's professional wit had deserted him. "It's nice to see you again," he said after an immense interval. "Shall we go and look at the aviary?"

"I hate to see birds in cages," said Marjorie, "and it's frightfully jolly just here. Do you think Mr. Wintersloan will paint this? He does paint, doesn't he?"

"I know him best in black and white," said Mr. Magnet.

Marjorie embarked on entirely insincere praises of Mr. Wintersloan's manner and personal effect; Magnet replied tepidly, with an air of reserving himself to grapple with the first conversational opportunity.

"It's a splendid day for tennis," said Marjorie. "I think I shall play tennis all the afternoon."

"I don't play well enough for this publicity."

"It's glorious exercise," said Marjorie. "Almost as good as dancing," and she decided to stick to that resolution. "I never lose a chance of tennis if I can help it."

She glanced round and detected a widening space between themselves and the next adjacent group.

"They're looking at the goldfish," she said. "Let us join them."

Everyone moved away as they came up to the little round pond, but then Marjorie had luck, and captured Prunella, and got her to hold hands and talk, until Fraulein Schmidt called the child away. And then Marjorie forced Mr. Magnet to introduce her to Mr. Bunford Paradise. She had a bright idea of sitting between Prunella and Mary at the lunch table, but a higher providence had assigned her to a seat at the end between Julia—or was it Kate?—and Mr. Magnet. However, one of the undergraduates was opposite, and she saved herself from undertones by talking across to him boldly about Newnham, though she hadn't an idea of his name or college. From that she came to tennis. To her inflamed imagination he behaved as if she was under a Taboo, but she was desperate, and had pledged him and his friend to a foursome before the meal was over.

"Don't you play?" said the undergraduate to Mr. Magnet.

"Very little," said Mr. Magnet. "Very little—"

At the end of an hour she was conspicuously and publicly shepherded from the tennis court by Mrs. Pope.

"Other people want to play," said her mother in a clear little undertone.

Mr. Magnet fielded her neatly as she came off the court.

"You play tennis like—a wild bird," he said, taking possession of her.

Only Marjorie's entire freedom from Irish blood saved him from a vindictive repartee.

§ 3

"Shall we go and look at the aviary?" said Mr. Magnet, reverting to a favourite idea of his, and then remembered she did not like to see caged birds.

"Perhaps we might see the Water Garden?" he said. "The Water Garden is really very delightful indeed—anyhow. You ought to see that."

On the spur of the moment, Marjorie could think of no objection to the Water Garden, and he led her off.

"I often think of that jolly walk we had last summer," said Mr. Magnet, "and how you talked about your work at Oxbridge."

Marjorie fell into a sudden rapture of admiration for a butterfly.

Twice more was Mr. Magnet baffled, and then they came to the little pool of water lilies with its miniature cascade of escape at the head and source of the Water Garden. "One of Lady Petchworth's great successes," said Mr. Magnet.

"I suppose the lotus is like the water-lily," said Marjorie, with no hope of staving off the inevitable——

She stood very still by the little pool, and in spite of her pensive regard of the floating blossoms, stiffly and intensely aware of his relentless regard.

"Marjorie," came his voice at last, strangely softened. "There is something I want to say to you."

She made no reply.

"Ever since we met last summer——"

A clear cold little resolution not to stand this, had established itself in Marjorie's mind. If she must decide, she would decide. He had brought it upon himself.

"Marjorie," said Mr. Magnet, "I love you."

She lifted a clear unhesitating eye to his face. "I'm sorry, Mr. Magnet," she said.

"I wanted to ask you to marry me," he said.

"I'm sorry, Mr. Magnet," she repeated.

They looked at one another. She felt a sort of scared exultation at having done it; her mother might say what she liked.

"I love you very much," he said, at a loss.

"I'm sorry," she repeated obstinately.

"I thought you cared for me a little."

She left that unanswered. She had a curious feeling that there was no getting away from this splashing, babbling pool, that she was fixed there until Mr. Magnet chose to release her, and that he didn't mean to release her yet. In which case she would go on refusing.

"I'm disappointed," he said.

Marjorie could only think that she was sorry again, but as she had already said that three times, she remained awkwardly silent.

"Is it because——" he began and stopped.

"It isn't because of anything. Please let's go back to the others, Mr. Magnet. I'm sorry if I'm disappointing."

And by a great effort she turned about.

Mr. Magnet remained regarding her—I can only compare it to the searching preliminary gaze of an artistic photographer. For a crucial minute in his life Marjorie hated him. "I don't understand," he said at last.

Then with a sort of naturalness that ought to have touched her he said: "Is it possible, Marjorie—that I might hope?—that I have been inopportune?"

She answered at once with absolute conviction.

"I don't think so, Mr. Magnet."

"I'm sorry," he said, "to have bothered you."

"I'm sorry," said Marjorie.

A long silence followed.

"I'm sorry too," he said.

They said no more, but began to retrace their steps. It was over. Abruptly, Mr. Magnet's bearing had become despondent—conspicuously despondent. "I had hoped," he said, and sighed.

With a thrill of horror Marjorie perceived he meant to look rejected, let every one see he had been rejected—after encouragement.

What would they think? How would they look?

What conceivably might they not say? Something of the importance of the thing she had done, became manifest to her. She felt first intimations of regret. They would all be watching, Mother, Daffy, Lady Petchworth. She would reappear with this victim visibly suffering beside her. What could she say to straighten his back and lift his chin? She could think of nothing. Ahead at the end of the shaded path she could see the copious white form, the agitated fair wig and red sunshade of Lady Petchworth——

§ 4

Mrs. Pope's eye was relentless; nothing seemed hidden from it; nothing indeed was hidden from it; Mr. Magnet's back was diagrammatic. Marjorie was a little flushed and bright-eyed, and professed herself eager, with an unnatural enthusiasm, to play golf-croquet. It was eloquently significant that Mr. Magnet did not share her eagerness, declined to play, and yet when she had started with the Rev. Jopling Baynes as partner, stood regarding the game with a sort of tender melancholy from the shade of the big chestnut-tree.

Mrs. Pope joined him unobtrusively.

"You're not playing, Mr. Magnet," she remarked.

"I'm a looker-on, this time," he said with a sigh.

"Marjorie's winning, I think," said Mrs. Pope.

He made no answer for some seconds.

"She looks so charming in that blue dress," he remarked at last, and sighed from the lowest deeps.

"That bird's-egg blue suits her," said Mrs. Pope, ignoring the sigh. "She's clever in her girlish way, she chooses all her own dresses,—colours, material, everything."

(And also, though Mrs. Pope had not remarked it, she concealed her bills.)

There came a still longer interval, which Mrs. Pope ended with the slightest of shivers. She perceived Mr. Magnet was heavy for sympathy and ripe to confide. "I think," she said, "it's a little cool here. Shall we walk to the Water Garden, and see if there are any white lilies?"

"There are," said Mr. Magnet sorrowfully, "and they are very beautiful—quite beautiful."

He turned to the path along which he had so recently led Marjorie.

He glanced back as they went along between Lady Petchworth's herbaceous border and the poppy beds. "She's so full of life," he said, with a sigh in his voice.

Mrs. Pope knew she must keep silent.

"I asked her to marry me this afternoon," Mr. Magnet blurted out. "I couldn't help it."

Mrs. Pope made her silence very impressive.

"I know I ought not to have done so without consulting you"—he went on lamely; "I'm very much in love with her. It's——It's done no harm."

Mrs. Pope's voice was soft and low. "I had no idea, Mr. Magnet.... You know she is very young. Twenty. A mother——"

"I know," said Magnet. "I can quite understand. But I've done no harm. She refused me. I shall go away to-morrow. Go right away for ever.... I'm sorry."

Another long silence.

"To me, of course, she's just a child," Mrs. Pope said at last. "She is only a child, Mr. Magnet. She could have had no idea that anything of the sort was in your mind——"

Her words floated away into the stillness.

For a time they said no more. The lilies came into sight, dreaming under a rich green shade on a limpid pool of brown water, water that slept and brimmed over as it were, unconsciously into a cool splash and ripple of escape. "How beautiful!" cried Mrs.

Pope, for a moment genuine.

"I spoke to her here," said Mr. Magnet.

The fountains of his confidence were unloosed.

"Now I've spoken to you about it, Mrs. Pope," he said, "I can tell you just how I—oh, it's the only word—adore her. She seems so sweet and easy—so graceful——"

Mrs. Pope turned on him abruptly, and grasped his hands; she was deeply moved. "I can't tell you," she said, "what it means to a mother to hear such things——"

Words failed her, and for some moments they engaged in a mutual pressure.

"Ah!" said Mr. Magnet, and had a queer wish it was the mother he had to deal with.

"Are you sure, Mr. Magnet," Mrs. Pope went on as their emotions subsided, "that she really meant what she said? Girls are very strange creatures——"

"She seems so clear and positive."

"Her manner is always clear and positive."

"Yes. I know."

"I know she has cared for you."

"No!"

"A mother sees. When your name used to be mentioned——. But these are not things to talk about. There is something—something sacred——"

"Yes," he said. "Yes. Only——Of course, one thing——"

Mrs. Pope seemed lost in the contemplation of water-lilies.

"I wondered," said Mr. Magnet, and paused again.

Then, almost breathlessly, "I wondered if there should be perhaps—some one else?"

She shook her head slowly. "I should know," she said.

"Are you sure?"

"I know I should know."

"Perhaps recently?"

"I am sure I should know. A mother's intuition——"

Memories possessed her for awhile. "A girl of twenty is a mass of contradictions. I can remember myself as if it was yesterday. Often one says no, or yes—out of sheer nervousness.... I am sure there is no other attachment——"

It occurred to her that she had said enough. "What a dignity that old gold-fish has!" she remarked. "He waves his tail—as if he were a beadle waving little boys out of church."

§ 5

Mrs. Pope astonished Marjorie by saying nothing about the all too obvious event of the day for some time, but her manner to her second daughter on their way home was strangely gentle. It was as if she had realized for the first time that regret and unhappiness might come into that young life. After supper, however, she spoke. They had all gone out just before the children went to bed to look for the new moon; Daffy was showing the pseudo-twins the old moon in the new moon's arms, and Marjorie found herself standing by her mother's side. "I hope dear," said Mrs. Pope, "that it's all for the best—and that you've done wisely, dear."

Marjorie was astonished and moved by her mother's tone.

"It's so difficult to know what is for the best," Mrs. Pope went on.

"I had to do—as I did," said Marjorie.

"I only hope you may never find you have made a Great Mistake, dear. He cares for you very, very much."

"Oh! we see it now!" cried Rom, "we see it now! Mummy, have you seen it? Like a little old round ghost being nursed!"

When Marjorie said "Good-night," Mrs. Pope kissed her with an unaccustomed effusion.

It occurred to Marjorie that after all her mother had no selfish end to serve in this affair.

§ 6

The idea that perhaps after all she had made a Great Mistake, the Mistake of her Life it might be, was quite firmly established in its place among all the other ideas in Marjorie's mind by the time she had dressed next morning. Subsequent events greatly intensified this persuasion. A pair of new stockings she had trusted sprang a bad hole as she put them on. She found two unmistakable bills from Oxbridge beside her plate, and her father was "horrid" at breakfast.

Her father, it appeared, had bought the ordinary shares of a Cuban railway very extensively, on the distinct understanding that they would improve. In a decent universe, with a proper respect for meritorious gentlemen, these shares would have improved accordingly, but the weather had seen fit to shatter the wisdom of Mr. Pope altogether. The sugar crop had collapsed, the bears were at work, and every morning now saw his nominal capital diminished by a dozen pounds or so. I do not know what Mr. Pope would have done if he had not had his family to help him bear his trouble. As it was he relieved his tension by sending Theodore from the table for dropping a knife, telling Rom when she turned the plate round to pick the largest banana that she hadn't the self-respect of a child of five, and remarking sharply from behind the Times when Daffy asked Marjorie if she was going to sketch: "Oh, for God's sake don't whisper!" Then when Mrs. Pope came round the table and tried to take his coffee cup softly to refill it without troubling him, he snatched at it, wrenched it roughly out of her hand, and said with his mouth full, and strangely in the manner of a snarling beast: "No' ready yet. Half foo'."

Marjorie wanted to know why every one didn't get up and leave the room. She glanced at her mother and came near to speaking.

And very soon she would have to come home and live in the midst of this again — indefinitely!

After breakfast she went to the tumbledown summer-house by the duckpond, and contemplated the bills she had not dared to open at table. One was boots, nearly three pounds, the other books, over seven. "I know that's wrong," said Marjorie, and rested her chin on her hand, knitted her brows and tried to remember the details of orders and deliveries....

Marjorie had fallen into the net prepared for our sons and daughters by the delicate modesty of the Oxbridge authorities in money matters, and she was, for her circumstances, rather heavily in debt. But I must admit that in Marjorie's nature the Oxbridge conditions had found an eager and adventurous streak that rendered her particularly apt to these temptations.

I doubt if reticence is really a virtue in a teacher.

But this is a fearful world, and the majority of those who instruct our youth have the painful sensitiveness of the cloistered soul to this spirit of terror in things. The young need particularly to be told truthfully and fully all we know of three fundamental things: the first of which is God, the next their duty towards their neighbours in the matter of work and money, and the third Sex. These things, and the adequate why of them, and some sort of adequate how, make all that matters in education. But all three are obscure and deeply moving topics, topics for which the donnish mind has a kind of special ineptitude, and which it evades with the utmost skill and delicacy. The middle part of this evaded triad was now being taken up in Marjorie's case by the Oxbridge tradespeople.

The Oxbridge shopkeeper is peculiar among shopkeepers in the fact that he has to do very largely with shy and immature customers with an extreme and distinctive ignorance of most commercial things. They are for the most part short of cash, but with vague and often large probabilities of credit behind them, for most people, even quite straitened people, will pull their sons and daughters out of altogether unreasonable debts at the end of their university career; and so the Oxbridge shopkeeper becomes a sort of propagandist of the charms and advantages of insolvency. Alone among retailers he dislikes the sight of cash, declines it, affects to regard it as a coarse ignorant truncation of a budding relationship, begs to be permitted to wait. So the youngster just up from home discovers that money may stay in the pocket, be used for cab and train fares and light refreshments; all the rest may be had for the asking. Marjorie, with her innate hunger for good fine things, with her quite insufficient pocket-money, and the irregular habits of expenditure a spasmodically financed, hard-up home is apt to engender, fell very readily into this new, delightful custom of having it put down (whatever it happened to be). She had all sorts of things put down. She and the elder Carmel girl used to go shopping together, having things put down. She brightened her rooms with colour-prints and engravings, got herself pretty and becoming clothes, acquired a fitted dressing-bag already noted in this story, and one or two other trifles of the sort, revised her foot-wear, created a very nice little bookshelf, and although at times she felt a little astonished and scared at herself, resolutely refused to estimate the total of accumulated debt she had attained. Indeed until the bills came in it was impossible to do that, because, following the splendid example of the Carmel girl, she hadn't even inquired the price of quite a number of things....

She didn't dare think now of the total. She lied even to herself about that. She had fixed on fifty pounds as the unendurable maximum. "It is less than fifty pounds," she said, and added: "must be." But something in her below the threshold of consciousness knew that it was more.

And now she was in her third year, and the Oxbridge tradesman, generally satisfied with the dimensions of her account, and no longer anxious to see it grow, was displaying the less obsequious side of his character. He wrote remarks at the bottom of his account, remarks about settlement, about having a bill to meet, about having something to go on with. He asked her to give the matter her "early attention." She had a disagreeable persuasion that if she wanted many more things anywhere she would have to pay ready money for them. She was particularly short of stockings. She had overlooked stockings recently.

Daffy, unfortunately, was also short of stockings.

And now, back with her family again, everything conspired to remind Marjorie of the old stringent habits from which she had had so delightful an interlude. She saw Daffy eye her possessions, reflect. This morning something of the awfulness of her position came to her....

At Oxbridge she had made rather a joke of her debts.

"I'd swear I haven't had three pairs of house shoes," said Marjorie. "But what can one do?"

And about the whole position the question was, "what can one do?"

She proceeded with tense nervous movements to tear these two distasteful demands into very minute pieces. Then she collected them all together in the hollow of her hand, and buried them in the loose mould in a corner of the summer-house.

"Madge," said Theodore, appearing in the sunshine of the doorway. "Aunt Plessington's coming! She's sent a wire. Someone's got to meet her by the twelve-forty train."

§ 7

Aunt Plessington's descent was due to her sudden discovery that Buryhamstreet was in close proximity to Summerhay Park, indeed only three miles away. She had promised a lecture on her movement for Lady Petchworth's village room in Summerhay, and she found that with a slight readjustment of dates she could combine this engagement with her promised visit to her husband's sister, and an evening or so of influence for her little Madge. So she had sent Hubert to telegraph at once, and "here," she said triumphantly on the platform, after a hard kiss at Marjorie's cheek, "we are again."

There, at any rate, she was, and Uncle Hubert was up the platform seeing after the luggage, in his small anxious way.

Aunt Plessington was a tall lean woman, with firm features, a high colour and a bright eye, who wore hats to show she despised them, and carefully dishevelled hair. Her dress was always good, but extremely old and grubby, and she commanded respect chiefly by her voice. Her voice was the true governing-class voice, a strangulated contralto, abundant and authoritative; it made everything she said clear and important, so that if she said it was a fine morning it was like leaded print in the Times, and she had over her large front teeth lips that closed quietly and with a slight effort after her speeches, as if the words she spoke tasted well and left a peaceful, secure sensation in the mouth.

Uncle Hubert was a less distinguished figure, and just a little reminiscent of the small attached husbands one finds among the lower crustacea: he was much shorter and rounder than his wife, and if he had been left to himself, he would probably have been comfortably fat in his quiet little way. But Aunt Plessington had made him a Haigite, which is one of the fiercer kinds of hygienist, just in the nick of time. He had round shoulders, a large nose, and glasses that made him look astonished—and she said he had a great gift for practical things, and made him see after everything in that line while she did the lecturing. His directions to the porter finished, he came up to his niece. "Hello, Marjorie!" he said, in a peculiar voice that sounded as though his mouth was full (though of course, poor dear, it wasn't), "how's the First Class?"

"A second's good enough for me, Uncle Hubert," said Marjorie, and asked if they would rather walk or go in the donkey cart, which was waiting outside with Daffy. Aunt Plessington, with an air of great bonhomie said she'd ride in the donkey cart, and they did. But no pseudo-twins or Theodore came to meet this arrival, as both uncle and aunt had a way of asking how the lessons were getting on that they found extremely disagreeable. Also, their aunt measured them, and incited them with loud encouraging noises to grow one against the other in an urgent, disturbing fashion.

Aunt Plessington's being was consumed by thoughts of getting on. She was like Bernard Shaw's life force, and she really did not seem to think there was anything in existence but shoving. She had no idea what a lark life can be, and occasionally how beautiful it can be when you do not shove, if only, which becomes increasingly hard each year, you can get away from the shovers. She was one of an energetic family of eight sisters who had maintained themselves against a mutual pressure by the use of their elbows from the cradle. They had all married against each other, all sorts of people; two had driven their husbands into bishoprics and made quite typical bishop's wives, one got a leading barrister, one a high war-office official, and one a rich Jew, and Aunt Plessington, after spending some years in just missing a rich and only slightly demented baronet, had pounced—it's the only word for it—on Uncle Hubert. "A woman is nothing without a husband," she said, and took him. He was a fairly comfortable Oxford don in his furtive way, and bringing him out and using him as a basis, she specialized in intellectual philanthropy and evolved her Movement. It was quite remarkable how rapidly she overhauled her sisters again.

What the Movement was, varied considerably from time to time, but it was always aggressively beneficial towards the lower strata of the community. Among its central ideas was her belief that these lower strata can no more be trusted to eat than they can to drink, and that the licensing monopoly which has made the poor man's beer thick, lukewarm and discreditable, and so greatly minimized its consumption, should be extended to the solid side of his dietary. She wanted to place considerable restrictions upon the sale of all sorts of meat, upon groceries and the less hygienic and more palatable forms of bread (which do not sufficiently stimulate the coatings of the stomach), to increase the present difficulties in the way of tobacco purchasers, and to put an end to that wanton and deleterious consumption of sweets which has so bad an effect upon the enamel of the teeth of the younger generation. Closely interwoven with these proposals was an adoption of the principle of the East Purblow Experiment, the principle of Payment in Kind. She was quite in agreement with Mr. Pope that poor people, when they had money, frittered it away, and so she proposed very extensive changes in the Truck Act, which could enable employers, under suitable safeguards, and with the advice of a small body of spinster inspectors, to supply hygienic housing, approved clothing of moral and wholesome sort, various forms of insurance, edifying rations, cuisine, medical aid and educational facilities as circumstances seemed to justify, in lieu of the wages the employees handled so ill....

As no people in England will ever admit they belong to the lower strata of society, Aunt Plessington's Movement attracted adherents from every class in the community.

She now, as they drove slowly to the vicarage, recounted to Marjorie—she had the utmost contempt for Daffy because of her irregular teeth and a general lack of progressive activity—the steady growth of the Movement, and the increasing respect shown for her and Hubert in the world of politico-social reform. Some of the meetings she had addressed had been quite full, various people had made various remarks about her, hostile for the most part and yet insidiously flattering, and everybody seemed quite glad to come to the little dinners she gave in order, she said, to gather social support for her reforms. She had been staying with the Mastersteins, who were keenly interested, and after she had polished off Lady Petchworth she was to visit Lady Rosenbaum. It was all going on swimmingly, these newer English gentry were eager to learn all she had to teach in the art of breaking in the Anglo-Saxon villagers, and now, how was Marjorie going on, and what was she going to do in the world?

Marjorie said she was working for her final.

"And what then?" asked Aunt Plessington.

"Not very clear, Aunt, yet."

"Looking around for something to take up?"

"Yes, Aunt."

"Well, you've time yet. And it's just as well to see how the land lies before you begin. It saves going back. You'll have to come up to London with me for a little while, and see things, and be seen a little."

"I should love to."

"I'll give you a good time," said Aunt Plessington, nodding promisingly. "Theodore getting on in school?"

"He's had his remove."

"And how's Sydney getting on with the music?"

"Excellently."

"And Rom. Rom getting on?"

Marjorie indicated a more restrained success.

"And what's Daffy doing?"

"Oh! get on!" said Daffy and suddenly whacked the donkey rather hard. "I beg your pardon, Aunt?"

"I asked what you were up to, Daffy?"

"Dusting, Aunt—and the virtues," said Daffy.

"You ought to find something better than that."

"Father tells me a lot about the East Purblow Experiment," said Daffy after a perceptible interval.

"Ah!" cried Aunt Plessington with a loud encouraging note, but evidently making the best of it, "that's better. Sociological observation."

"Yes, Aunt," said Daffy, and negotiated a corner with exceptional care.

§ 8

Mrs. Pope, who had an instinctive disposition to pad when Aunt Plessington was about, had secured the presence at lunch of Mr. Magnet (who was after all staying on in Buryhamstreet) and the Rev. Jopling Baynes. Aunt Plessington liked to meet the clergy, and would always if she could win them over to an interest in the Movement. She opened the meal with a brisk attack upon him. "Come, Mr. Baynes," she said, "what do your people eat here? Hubert and I are making a study of the gluttonous side of village life, and we find that no one knows so much of that as the vicar—not even the doctor."

The Reverend Jopling Baynes was a clergyman of the evasive type with a quite distinguished voice. He pursed his lips and made his eyes round. "Well, Mrs. Plessington," he said and fingered his glass, "it's the usual dietary. The usual dietary."

"Too much and too rich, badly cooked and eaten too fast," said Aunt Plessington. "And what do you think is the remedy?"

"We make an Effort," said the Rev. Jopling Baynes, "we make an Effort. A Hint here, a Word there."

"Nothing organized?"

"No," said the Rev. Jopling Baynes, and shook his head with a kind of resignation.

"We are going to alter all that," said Aunt Plessington briskly, and went on to expound the Movement and the diverse way in which it might be possible to control and improve the domestic expenditure of the working classes.

The Rev. Jopling Baynes listened sympathetically across the table and tried to satisfy a healthy appetite with as abstemious an air as possible while he did so. Aunt Plessington passed rapidly from general principles, to a sketch of the success of the movement, and Hubert, who had hitherto been busy with his lunch, became audible from behind the exceptionally large floral trophy that concealed him from his wife, bubbling confirmatory details. She was very bright and convincing as she told of this prominent man met and subdued, that leading antagonist confuted, and how the Bishops were coming in. She made it clear in her swift way that an intelligent cleric resolved to get on in this world en route for a better one hereafter, might do worse than take up her Movement. And this touched in, she turned her mind to Mr. Magnet.

(That floral trophy, I should explain, by the by, was exceptionally large because of Mrs. Pope's firm conviction that Aunt Plessington starved her husband. Accordingly, she masked him, and so was able to heap second and third helpings upon his plate without Aunt Plessington discovering his lapse. The avidity with which Hubert ate confirmed her worst suspicions and evinced, so far as anything ever did evince, his gratitude.)

"Well, Mr. Magnet," she said, "I wish I had your sense of humour."

"I wish you had," said Mr. Magnet.

"I should write tracts," said Aunt Plessington.

"I knew it was good for something," said Mr. Magnet, and Daffy laughed in a tentative way.

"I mean it," said Aunt Plessington brightly. "Think if we had a Dickens—and you are the nearest man alive to Dickens—on the side of social reform to-day!"

Mr. Magnet's light manner deserted him. "We do what we can, Mrs. Plessington," he said.

"How much more might be done," said Aunt Plessington, "if humour could be organized."

"Hear, hear!" said Mr. Pope.

"If all the humorists of England could be induced to laugh at something together."

"They do—at times," said Mr. Magnet, but the atmosphere was too serious for his light touch.

"They could laugh it out of existence," said Aunt Plessington.

It was evident Mr. Magnet was struck by the idea.

"Of course," he said, "in Punch, to which I happen to be an obscure occasional contributor——"

Mrs. Pope was understood to protest that he should not say such things.

"We do remember just what we can do either in the way of advertising or injury. I don't think you'll find us up against any really solid institutions."

"But do you think, Mr. Magnet, you are sufficiently kind to the New?" Aunt Plessington persisted.

"I think we are all grateful to Punch," said the Rev. Jopling Baynes suddenly and sonorously, "for its steady determination to direct our mirth into the proper channels. I do not think that any one can accuse its editor of being unmindful of his great responsibilities——"

Marjorie found it a very interesting conversation.

She always met her aunt again with a renewal of a kind of admiration. That loud authoritative rudeness, that bold thrusting forward of the Movement until it became the sole criterion of worth or success, this annihilation by disregard of all that Aunt Plessington wasn't and didn't and couldn't, always in the intervals seemed too good to be true. Of course this really was the way people got on and made a mark, but she felt it must be almost as trying to the nerves as aeronautics. Suppose, somewhere up there your engine stopped! How Aunt Plessington dominated the table! Marjorie tried not to catch Daffy's eye. Daffy was unostentatiously keeping things going, watching the mustard, rescuing the butter, restraining Theodore, and I am afraid not listening very carefully to Aunt Plessington. The children were marvellously silent and jumpily well-behaved, and Mr. Pope, in a very unusual state of subdued amiability, sat at the end of the table with the East Purblow experiment on the tip of his tongue. He liked Aunt Plessington, and she was good for him. They had the same inherent distrust of the intelligence and good intentions of their fellow creatures, and she had the knack of making him feel that he too was getting on, that she was saying things on his behalf in influential quarters, and in spite of the almost universal conspiracy (based on jealousy) to ignore his stern old-world virtues, he might still be able to battle his way to the floor of the House of Commons and there deliver himself before he died of a few sorely needed home-truths about motor cars, decadence and frivolity generally....

§ 9

After lunch Aunt Plessington took her little Madge for an energetic walk, and showed herself far more observant than the egotism of her conversation at that meal might have led one to suppose. Or perhaps she was only better informed. Aunt Plessington loved a good hard walk in the afternoon; and if she could get any one else to accompany her, then Hubert stayed at home, and curled up into a ball on a sofa somewhere, and took a little siesta that made him all the brighter for the intellectual activities of the evening. The thought of a young life, new, untarnished, just at the outset, just addressing itself to the task of getting on, always stimulated her mind extremely, and she talked to Marjorie with a very real and effectual desire to help her to the utmost of her ability.

She talked of a start in life, and the sort of start she had had. She showed how many people who began with great advantages did not shove sufficiently, and so dropped out of things and weren't seen and mentioned. She defended herself for marrying Hubert, and showed what a clever shoving thing it had been to do. It startled people a little, and made them realize that here was a woman who wanted something more in a man than a handsome organ-grinder. She made it clear that she thought a clever marriage, if not a startlingly brilliant one, the first duty of a girl. It was a girl's normal gambit. She branched off to the things single women might do, in order to justify this view. She did not think single women could do very much. They might perhaps shove as suffragettes, but even there a husband helped tremendously—if only by refusing to bail you out. She ran over the cases of a number of prominent single women.

"And what," said Aunt Plessington, "do they all amount to? A girl is so hampered and an old maid is so neglected," said Aunt Plessington.

She paused.

"Why don't you up and marry Mr. Magnet, Marjorie?" she said, with her most brilliant flash.

"It takes two to make a marriage, aunt," said Marjorie after a slight hesitation.

"My dear child! he worships the ground you tread on!" said Aunt Plessington.

"He's rather—grown up," said Marjorie.

"Not a bit of it. He's not forty. He's just the age."

"I'm afraid it's a little impossible."

"Impossible?"

"You see I've refused him, aunt."

"Naturally—the first time! But I wouldn't send him packing the second."

There was an interval.

Marjorie decided on a blunt question. "Do you really think, aunt, I should do well to marry Mr. Magnet?"

"He'd give you everything a clever woman needs," said Aunt Plessington. "Everything."

With swift capable touches she indicated the sort of life the future Mrs. Magnet might enjoy. "He's evidently a man who wants helping to a position," she said. "Of course his farces and things, I'm told, make no end of money, but he's just a crude gift by himself. Money like that is nothing. With a clever wife he might be all sorts of things. Without one he'll just subside—you know the sort of thing this sort of man does. A rather eccentric humorous house in the country, golf, croquet, horse-riding, rose-growing, queer hats."

"Isn't that rather what he would like to do, aunt?" said Marjorie.

"That's not our business, Madge," said Aunt Plessington with humorous emphasis.

She began to sketch out a different and altogether smarter future for the fortunate humorist. There would be a house in a good central position in London where Marjorie would have bright successful lunches and dinners, very unpretending and very good, and tempt the clever smart with the lure of the interestingly clever; there would be a bright little country cottage in some pretty accessible place to which Aunt and Uncle Plessington and able and influential people generally could be invited for gaily recreative and yet extremely talkative and helpful week-ends. Both places could be made centres of intrigue; conspiracies for getting on and helping and exchanging help could be organized, people could be warned against people whose getting-on was undesirable. In the midst of it all, dressed with all the natural wit she had and an enlarging experience, would be Marjorie, shining like a rising planet. It wouldn't be long, if she did things well, before she had permanent officials and young cabinet ministers mingling with her salad of writers and humorists and the Plessington connexion.

"Then," said Aunt Plessington with a joyous lift in her voice, "you'll begin to weed a little."

For a time the girl's mind resisted her.

But Marjorie was of the impressionable sex at an impressionable age, and there was something overwhelming in the undeviating conviction of her aunt, in the clear assurance of her voice, that this life which interested her was the real life, the only possible successful life. The world reformed itself in Marjorie's fluent mind, until it was all a scheme of influence and effort and ambition and triumphs. Dinner-parties and receptions, men wearing orders, cabinet ministers more than a little in love asking her advice, beautiful robes, a great blaze of lights; why! she might be, said Aunt Plessington rising to enthusiasm, "another Marcella." The life was not without its adventurous side; it wasn't in any way dull. Aunt Plessington to illustrate that point told amusing anecdotes of how two almost impudent invitations on her part had succeeded, and how she had once scored off her elder sister by getting a coveted celebrity through their close family resemblance. "After accepting he couldn't very well refuse because I wasn't somebody else," she ended gleefully. "So he came—and stayed as long as anybody."

What else was there for Marjorie to contemplate? If she didn't take this by no means unattractive line, what was the alternative? Some sort of employment after a battle with her father, a parsimonious life, and even then the Oxbridge tradesmen and their immortal bills....

Aunt Plessington was so intent upon her theme that she heeded nothing of the delightful little flowers she trampled under foot across the down, nor the jolly squirrel with an artistic temperament who saw fit to give an uninvited opinion upon her personal appearance from the security of a beech-tree in the wood. But Marjorie, noting quite a number of such things with the corner of her mind, and being now well under the Plessington sway, wished she had more concentration....

In the evening after supper the customary games were suspended, and Mr. and Mrs. Plessington talked about getting on, and work and efficiency generally, and explained how so-and-so had spoilt his chances in life, and why so-and-so was sure to achieve nothing, and how this man ate too much and that man drank too much, and on the contrary what promising and capable people the latest adherents of and subscribers to the Movement were, until two glasses of hot water came—Aunt Plessington had been told it was good for her digestion and she thought it just as well that Hubert should have some too—and it was time for every one to go to bed.

§ 10

Next morning an atmosphere of getting on and strenuosity generally prevailed throughout the vicarage. The Plessingtons were preparing a memorandum on their movement for the "Reformer's Year Book," every word was of importance and might win or lose adherents and subscribers, and they secured the undisturbed possession of the drawing-room, from which the higher notes of Aunt Plessington's voice explaining the whole thing to Hubert, who had to write it out, reached, a spur to effort, into every part of the house.

Their influence touched every one.

Marjorie, struck by the idea that she was not perhaps getting on at Oxbridge so fast as she ought to do, went into the summer-house with Marshall's "Principles of Economics," read for two hours, and did not think about her bills for more than a quarter of the time. Rom, who had already got up early and read through about a third of "Aurora Leigh," now set herself with dogged determination to finish that great poem. Syd practised an extra ten minutes—for Aunt Plessington didn't mind practice so long as there wasn't a tune. Mrs. Pope went into the kitchen and made a long-needed fuss about the waste of rice. Mr. Pope began the pamphlet he had had in contemplation for some time upon the advantages to public order of Payment in Kind. Theodore, who had washed behind his ears and laced his boots in all the holes, went into the yard before breakfast and hit a tennis ball against the wall and back, five hundred and twenty-two times—a record. He would have resumed this after breakfast, but his father came round the corner of the house with a pen in his mouth, and asked him indistinctly, but fiercely, what the devil he was doing. So he went away, and after a fretful interval set himself to revise his Latin irregular verbs. By twelve he had done wonders.

Later in the day the widening circle of aggressive urgency reached the kitchen, and at two the cook gave notice in order, she said, to better herself.

Lunch, unconscious of this impending shadow, was characterized by a virtuous cheerfulness, and Aunt Plessington told in detail how her seven and twenty nephews and nieces, the children of her various sisters, were all getting on. On the whole, they were not getting on so brilliantly as they might have done (which indeed is apt to be the case with the children of people who have loved not well but too wisely), and it was borne in upon the mind of the respectfully listening Marjorie that, to borrow an easy colloquialism of her aunt's, she might "take the shine out of the lot of them" with a very little zeal and effort—and of course Mr. Magnet.

The lecture in the evening at Summerhay was a great success.

The chair was taken by the Rev. Jopling Baynes, Lady Petchworth was enthroned behind the table, Hubert was in charge of his wife's notes—if notes should be needed—and Mr. Pope, expectant of an invitation at the end to say a few words about the East Purblow experiment, also occupied a chair on the platform. Lady Petchworth, with her abundant soft blond hair, brightly blond still in spite of her fifty-five years, her delicate features, her plump hands, her numerous chins and her entirely inaudible voice, made a pleasing contrast with Aunt Plessington's resolute personality. She had perhaps an even greater assurance of authority, but it was a quiet assurance; you felt that she knew that if she spoke in her sleep she would be obeyed, that it was quite unnecessary to make herself heard. The two women, indeed, the one so assertive, the other so established, were at the opposite poles of authoritative British womanhood, and harmonized charmingly. The little room struck the note of a well-regulated brightness at every point, it had been decorated in a Keltic but entirely respectful style by one of Lady Petchworth's artistic discoveries, it was lit by paraffin lamps that smelt hardly at all, and it was gay with colour prints illustrating the growth of the British Empire from the battle of Ethandune to the surrender of Cronje. The hall was fairly full. Few could afford to absent themselves from these brightening occasions, but there was a tendency on the part of the younger and the less thoughtful section of the village manhood to accumulate at the extreme back and rumble in what appeared to be a slightly ironical spirit, so far as it had any spirit, with its feet.

The Rev. Jopling Baynes opened proceedings with a few well-chosen remarks, in which he complimented every one present either singly or collectively according to their rank and importance, and then Aunt Plessington came forward to the centre of the platform amidst a hectic flush of applause, and said "Haw!" in a loud clear ringing tone.

She spoke without resorting to the notes in Hubert's little fist, very freely and easily. Her strangulated contralto went into every corner of the room and positively seemed to look for and challenge inattentive auditors. She had come over, she said, and she had been very glad to come over and talk to them that night, because it meant not only seeing them but meeting her very dear delightful friend Lady Petchworth (loud applause) and staying for a day or so with her brother-in-law Mr. Pope (unsupported outburst of applause from Mr. Magnet), to whom she and social reform generally owed so much. She had come to talk to them that night about the National Good Habits Movement, which was attracting so much attention and which bore so closely on our National Life and Character; she happened to be—here Aunt Plessington smiled as she spoke—a humble person connected with that movement, just a mere woman connected with it; she was going to explain to them as well as she could in her womanly way and in the time at her disposal just what it was and just what it was for, and just what means it adopted and just what ends it had in view. Well, they all knew what Habits were, and that there were Good Habits and Bad Habits, and she supposed that the difference between a good man and a bad man was just that the good man had good habits and the bad one had bad habits. Everybody she supposed wanted to get on. If a man had good habits he got on, and if he had bad habits he didn't get on, and she supposed it was the same with a country, if its people had good habits they got on, and if its people had bad habits they didn't get on. For her own part she and her husband (Hubert gave a little self-conscious jump) had always cultivated good habits, and she had to thank him with all her heart for his help in doing so. (Applause from the front seats.) Now, the whole idea of her movement was to ask, how can we raise the standard of the national habits? how can we get rid of bad habits and cultivate good ones?... (Here there was a slight interruption due to some one being suddenly pushed off the end of a form at the back, and coming to the floor with audible violence, after which a choked and obstructed tittering continued intermittently for some time.)

Some of her audience, she remarked, had not yet acquired the habit of sitting still.

(Laughter, and a coarse vulgar voice: "Good old Billy Punt!")

Well, to resume, she and her husband had made a special and careful study of habits; they had consulted all sorts of people and collected all sorts of statistics, in fact they had devoted themselves to this question, and the conclusion to which they came was this, that Good Habits were acquired by Training and Bad Habits came from neglect and carelessness and leaving people, who weren't fit for such freedom, to run about and do just whatever they liked. And so, she went on with a note of complete demonstration, the problem resolved itself into the question of how far they could get more Training into the national life, and how they could check extravagant and unruly and wasteful and unwise ways of living. (Hear, hear! from Mr. Pope.) And this was the problem she and her husband had set themselves to solve.

(Scuffle, and a boy's voice at the back, saying: "Oh, shut it, Nuts! Shut it!")

Well, she and her husband had worked the thing out, and they had come to the conclusion that what was the matter with the great mass of English people was first that they had rather too much loose money, and secondly that they had rather too much loose time. (A voice: "What O!" and the Rev. Jopling Baynes suddenly extended his neck, knitted his brows, and became observant of the interrupter.) She did not say they had too much money (a second voice: "Not Arf!"), but too much loose money. She did not say they had too much time but too much loose time, that is to say, they had money and time they did not know how to spend properly. And so they got into mischief. A great number of people in this country, she maintained, and this was especially true of the lower classes, did not know how to spend either money or time; they bought themselves wasteful things and injurious things, and they frittered away their hours in all sorts of foolish, unprofitable ways. And, after the most careful and scientific study of this problem, she and her husband had come to the conclusion that two main principles must underlie any remedial measures that were attempted, the first of which was the Principle of Payment in Kind, which had already had so interesting a trial at the great carriage works of East Purblow, and the second, the Principle of Continuous Occupation, which had been recognized long ago in popular wisdom by that admirable proverb—or rather quotation—she believed it was a quotation, though she gave, she feared, very little time to poetry ("Better employed," from Mr. Pope)—

> "Satan finds some mischief still
> For idle hands to do."

(Irrepressible outbreak of wild and sustained applause from the back seats, and in a sudden lull a female voice asking in a flattened, thwarted tone: "Ain't there to be no lantern then?")

The lecturer went on to explain what was meant by either member of what perhaps they would permit her to call this double-barrelled social remedy.

It was an admirable piece of lucid exposition. Slowly the picture of a better, happier, more disciplined England grew upon the minds of the meeting. First she showed the new sort of employer her movement would evoke, an employer paternal, philanthropic, vaguely responsible for the social order of all his dependants. (Lady Petchworth was seen to nod her head slowly at this.) Only in the last resort, and when he was satisfied that his worker and his worker's family were properly housed, hygienically clothed and fed, attending suitable courses of instruction and free from any vicious inclinations, would he pay wages in cash. In the discharge of the duties of payment he would have the assistance of expert advice, and the stimulus of voluntary inspectors of his own class. He would be the natural clan-master, the captain and leader, adviser and caretaker of his banded employees. Responsibility would stimulate him, and if responsibility did not stimulate him, inspectors (both men and women inspectors) would. The worker, on the other hand, would be enormously more healthy and efficient under the new régime. His home, designed by qualified and officially recognized architects, would be prettier as well as more convenient and elevating to his taste, his children admirably trained and dressed in the new and more beautiful clothing with which Lady Petchworth (applause) had done so much to make them familiar, his vital statistics compared with current results would be astonishingly good, his mind free from any anxiety but the proper anxiety of a man in his position, to get his work done properly and earn recognition from those competent and duly authorized to judge it. Of all this she spoke with the inspiring note of absolute conviction. All this would follow Payment in Kind and Continuous Occupation as days follow sunrise. And there would always,—and here Aunt Plessington's voice seemed to brighten—be something for the worker to get on with, something for him to do; lectures, classes, reading-rooms, improving entertainments. His time would be filled. The proper authorities would see that it was filled—and filled in the right way. Never for a moment need he be bored. He would never have an excuse for being bored. That was the second great idea, the complementary idea to the first. "And here it is," she said, turning a large encouraging smile on Lady Petchworth, "that the work of a National Theatre, instructive, stimulating, well regulated, and morally sustaining, would come in." He wouldn't, of course, be compelled to go, but there would be his seat, part of his payment in kind, and the public-house would be shut, most other temptations would be removed....

The lecture reached its end at last with only one other interruption. Some would-be humorist suddenly inquired, à propos of nothing: "What's the fare to America, Billy?" and a voice, presumably Billy's, answered him: "Mor'n you'll ev 'av in you' pocket."

The Rev. Jopling Baynes, before he called upon Mr. Pope for his promised utterance about East Purblow, could not refrain from pointing out how silly "in every sense of the word" these wanton interruptions were. What, he asked, had English social reform to do with the fare to America?—and having roused the meeting to an alert silence by the length of his pause, answered in a voice of ringing contempt: "Nothing— whatsoever." Then Mr. Pope made his few remarks about East Purblow with the ease and finish that comes from long practice; much, he said, had to be omitted "in view of" the restricted time at his disposal, but he did not grudge that, the time had been better filled. ("No, no," from Aunt Plessington.) Yes, yes,—by the lucid and delightful lecture they had all enjoyed, and he not least among them. (Applause.)...

§ 11

They came out into a luminous blue night, with a crescent young moon high overhead. It was so fine that the Popes and the Plessingtons and Mr. Magnet declined Lady Petchworth's proffered car, and walked back to Buryhamstreet across the park through a sleeping pallid cornfield, and along by the edge of the pine woods. Mr. Pope would have liked to walk with Mr. Magnet and explain all that the pressure on his time had caused him to omit from his speech, and why it was he had seen fit to omit this part and include that. Some occult power, however, baffled this intention, and he found himself going home in the company of his brother-in-law and Daffy, with Aunt Plessington and his wife like a barrier between him and his desire. Marjorie, on the other hand, found Mr. Magnet's proximity inevitable. They fell a little behind and were together again for the first time since her refusal.

He behaved, she thought, with very great restraint, and indeed he left her a little doubtful on that occasion whether he had not decided to take her decision as final. He talked chiefly about the lecture, which had impressed him very deeply. Mrs. Plessington, he said, was so splendid—made him feel trivial. He felt stirred up by her, wanted to help in this social work, this picking up of helpless people from the muddle in which they wallowed.

He seemed not only extraordinarily modest but extraordinarily gentle that night, and the warm moonshine gave his face a shadowed earnestness it lacked in more emphatic lights. She felt the profound change in her feelings towards him that had followed her rejection of him. It had cleared away his effect of oppression upon her. She had no longer any sense of entanglement and pursuit, and all the virtues his courtship had obscured shone clear again. He was kindly, he was patient—and she felt something about him a woman is said always to respect, he gave her an impression of ability. After all, he could banish the trouble that crushed and overwhelmed her with a movement of his little finger. Of all her load of debt he could earn the payment in a day.

"Your aunt goes to-morrow?" he said.

Marjorie admitted it.

"I wish I could talk to her more. She's so inspiring."

"You know of our little excursion for Friday?" he asked after a pause.

She had not heard. Friday was Theodore's birthday; she knew it only too well because she had had to part with her stamp collection—which very luckily had chanced to get packed and come to Buryhamstreet—to meet its demand. Mr. Magnet explained he had thought it might be fun to give a picnic in honour of the anniversary.

"How jolly of you!" said Marjorie.

"There's a pretty bit of river between Wamping and Friston Hanger—I've wanted you to see it for a long time, and Friston Hanger church has the prettiest view. The tower gets the bend of the river."

He told her all he meant to do as if he submitted his plans for her approval. They would drive to Wamping and get a very comfortable little steam launch one could hire there. Wintersloan was coming down again; an idle day of this kind just suited his temperament. Theodore would like it, wouldn't he?

"Theodore will think he is King of Surrey!"

"I'll have a rod and line if he wants to fish. I don't want to forget anything. I want it to be his day really and truly."

The slightest touch upon the pathetic note? She could not tell.

But that evening brought Marjorie nearer to loving Magnet than she had ever been. Before she went to sleep that night she had decided he was quite a tolerable person again; she had been too nervous and unjust with him. After all, his urgency and awkwardness had been just a part of his sincerity. Perhaps the faint doubt whether he would make his request again gave the zest of uncertainty to his devotion. Of course, she told herself, he would ask again. And then the blissful air of limitless means she might breathe. The blessed release....

She was suddenly fast asleep.

§ 12

Friday was after all not so much Theodore's day as Mr. Magnet's.

Until she found herself committed there was no shadow of doubt in Marjorie's mind of what she meant to do. "Before I see you again," said Aunt Plessington at the parting kiss, "I hope you'll have something to tell me." She might have been Hymen thinly disguised as an aunt, waving from the departing train. She continued by vigorous gestures and unstinted display of teeth and a fluttering handkerchief to encourage Marjorie to marry Mr. Magnet, until the curve of the cutting hid her from view....

Fortune favoured Mr. Magnet with a beautiful day, and the excursion was bright and successful from the outset. It was done well, and what perhaps was more calculated to impress Marjorie, it was done with lavish generosity. From the outset she turned a smiling countenance upon her host. She did her utmost to suppress a reviving irrational qualm in her being, to maintain clearly and simply her overnight decision, that he should propose again and that she should accept him.

Yet the festival was just a little dreamlike in its quality to her perceptions. She found she could not focus clearly on its details.

Two waggonettes came from Wamping; there was room for everybody and to spare, and Wamping revealed itself a pleasant small country town with stocks under the market hall, and just that tint of green paint and that loafing touch the presence of a boating river gives.

The launch was brilliantly smart with abundant crimson cushions and a tasselled awning, and away to the left was a fine old bridge that dated in its essentials from Plantagenet times.

They started with much whistling and circling, and went away up river under overhanging trees that sometimes swished the funnel, splashing the meadow path and making the reeds and bulrushes dance with their wash. They went through a reluctant lock, steamed up a long reach, they passed the queerly painted Potwell Inn with its picturesque group of poplars and its absurd new notice-board of "Omlets." ... Theodore was five stone of active happiness; he and the pseudo-twins, strictly under his orders as the universal etiquette of birthdays prescribes, clambered round and round the boat, clutching the awning rail and hanging over the water in an entirely secure and perilous looking manner. No one, unless his father happened to be upset by something, would check him, he knew, on this auspicious day. Mr. Magnet sat with the grey eye on Marjorie and listened a little abstractedly to Mr. Pope, who was telling very fully what he would say if the Liberal party were to ask his advice at the present juncture. Mrs. Pope attended discreetly, and Daffy and Marjorie with a less restrained interest, to Mr. Wintersloan, who showed them how to make faces out of a fist tied up in a pocket-handkerchief, how to ventriloquize, how to conjure with halfpence—which he did very amusingly—and what the buttons on a man's sleeve were for; Theodore clambering at his back discovered what he was at, and by right of birthday made him do all the faces and tricks over again. Then Mr. Wintersloan told stories of all the rivers along which, he said, he had travelled in steamboats; the Rhine, the Danube, the Hoogly and the Fall River, and particularly how he had been bitten by a very young crocodile. "It's the smell of the oil brings it all back to me," he said. "And the kind of sway it gives you."

He made sinuous movements of his hand, and looked at Marjorie with that wooden yet expressive smile.

Friston Hanger proved to be even better than Wamping. It had a character of its own because it was built very largely of a warm buff coloured local rock instead of the usual brick, and the outhouses at least of the little inn at which they landed were thatched. Most of the cottages had casement windows with diamond panes, and the streets were cobbled and very up-and-down hill. The place ran to high walls richly suggestive of hidden gardens, overhung by big trees and pierced by secretive important looking doors. And over it all rose an unusually big church, with a tall buttressed tower surmounted by a lantern of pierced stone.

"We'll go through the town and look at the ruins of the old castle beyond the church," said Mr. Magnet to Marjorie, "and then I want you to see the view from the church tower."

And as they went through the street, he called her attention again to the church tower in a voice that seemed to her to be inexplicably charged with significance. "I want you to go up there," he said.

"How about something to eat, Mr. Magnet?" remarked Theodore suddenly, and everybody felt a little surprised when Mr. Magnet answered: "Who wants things to eat on your birthday, Theodore?"

But they saw the joke of that when they reached the castle ruins and found in the old tilting yard, with its ivy-covered arch framing a view of the town and stream, a table spread with a white cloth that shone in the sunshine, glittering with glass and silver and gay with a bowl of salad and flowers and cold pies and a jug of claret-cup and an ice pail—a silver pail! containing two promising looking bottles, in the charge of two real live waiters, in evening dress as waiters should be, but with straw hats to protect them from the sun and weather. "Oh!" cried Mrs. Pope, "what a splendid idea, Mr. Magnet," when the destination of the feast was perfectly clear, and even Theodore seemed a little overawed—almost as if he felt his birthday was being carried too far and might provoke a judgment later. Manifestly Mr. Magnet must have ordered this in London, and have had it sent down, waiters and all! Theodore knew he was a very wonderful little boy in spite of the acute criticism of four devoted sisters, and Mr. Magnet had noticed him before at times, but this was, well, rather immense! "Look at the pie-crusts, old man!" And on the pie-crusts, and on the icing of the cake, their munificent host had caused to be done in little raised letters of dough and chocolate the word "Theodore."

"Oh, Mr. Magnet!" said Marjorie—his eye so obviously invited her to say something. Mr. Pope tried a nebulous joke about "groaning boards of Frisky Hanger," and only Mr. Wintersloan restrained his astonishment and admiration. "You could have got those chaps in livery," he said—unheeded. The lunch was as a matter of fact his idea; he had refused to come unless it was provided, and he had somehow counted on blue coats, brass buttons, and yellow waistcoats—but everybody else of course ascribed the whole invention to Mr. Magnet.

"Well," said Mr. Pope with a fine air of epigram, "the only thing I can say is—to eat it," and prepared to sit down.

"Melon," cried Mr. Magnet to the waiters, "we'll begin with the melon. Have you ever tried melon with pepper and salt, Mrs. Pope?"

"You put salt in everything," admired Mr. Pope.

"Salt from those attics of yours—Attic salt."

"Or there's ginger!" said Mr. Magnet, after a whisper from the waiter.

Mr. Pope said something classical about "ginger hot in the mouth."

"Some of these days," said Mr. Wintersloan, "when I have exhausted all other sensations, I mean to try melon and mustard."

Rom made a wonderful face at him.

"I can think of worse things than that," said Mr. Wintersloan with a hard brightness.

"Not till after lunch, Mr. Wintersloan!" said Rom heartily.

"The claret cup's all right for Theodore, Mrs. Pope," said Magnet. "It's a special twelve year old brand." (He thought of everything!)

"Mummy," said Mr. Pope. "You'd better carve this pie, I think."

"I want very much," said Mr. Magnet in Marjorie's ear and very confidentially, "to show you the view from the church tower. I think—it will appeal to you."

"Rom!" said Theodore, uncontrollably, in a tremendous stage whisper. "There's peaches!... There! on the hamper!"

"Champagne, m'am?" said the waiter suddenly in Mrs. Pope's ear, wiping ice-water from the bottle.

(But what could it have cost him?)

§ 13

Marjorie would have preferred that Mr. Magnet should not have decided with such relentless determination to make his second proposal on the church tower. His purpose was luminously clear to her from the beginning of lunch onward, and she could feel her nerves going under the strain of that long expectation. She tried to pull herself together, tried not to think about it, tried to be amused by the high spirits and nonsense of Mr. Wintersloan and Syd and Rom and Theodore; but Mr. Magnet was very pervasive, and her mother didn't ever look at her, looked past her and away from her and all round her, in a profoundly observant manner. Marjorie felt chiefly anxious to get to the top of that predestinate tower and have the whole thing over, and it was with a start that she was just able to prevent one of the assiduous waiters filling her glass with champagne for the third time.

There was a little awkwardness in dispersing after lunch. Mr. Pope, his heart warmed by the champagne and mellowed by a subsequent excellent cigar, wanted very much to crack what he called a "postprandial jest" or so with the great humorist, while

Theodore also, deeply impressed with the discovery that there was more in Mr. Magnet than he had supposed, displayed a strong disposition to attach himself more closely than he had hitherto done to this remarkable person, and study his quiet but enormous possibilities with greater attention. Mrs. Pope with a still alertness did her best to get people adjusted, but Syd and Rom had conceived a base and unnatural desire to subjugate the affections of the youngest waiter, and wouldn't listen to her proposal that they should take Theodore away into the town; Mr. Wintersloan displayed extraordinary cunning and resource in evading a tête-à-tête with Mr. Pope that would have released Mr. Magnet. Now Mrs. Pope came to think of it, Mr. Wintersloan never had had the delights of a good talk with Mr. Pope, he knew practically nothing about the East Purblow experiment except for what Mr. Magnet might have retailed to him, and she was very greatly puzzled to account for his almost manifest reluctance to go into things thoroughly. Daffy remained on hand, available but useless, and Mrs. Pope, smiling at the landscape and a prey to Management within, was suddenly inspired to take her eldest daughter into her confidence. "Daffy," she said, with a guileful finger extended and pointing to the lower sky as though she was pointing out the less obvious and more atmospheric beauties of Surrey, "get Theodore away from Mr. Magnet if you can. He wants to talk to Marjorie."

Daffy looked round. "Shall I call him?" she said.

"No," said Mrs. Pope, "do it—just—quietly."

"I'll try," said Daffy and stared at her task, and Mrs. Pope, feeling that this might or might not succeed but that anyhow she had done what she could, strolled across to her husband and laid a connubial touch upon his shoulder. "All the young people," she said, "are burning to climb the church tower. I never can understand this activity after lunch."

"Not me," said Mr. Pope. "Eh, Magnet?"

"I'm game," said Theodore. "Come along, Mr. Magnet."

"I think," said Mr. Magnet looking at Marjorie, "I shall go up. I want to show Marjorie the view."

"We'll stay here, Mummy, eh?" said Mr. Pope, with a quite unusual geniality, and suddenly put his arm round Mrs. Pope's waist. Her motherly eye sought Daffy's, and indicated her mission. "I'll come with you, Theodore," said Daffy. "There isn't room for everyone at once up that tower."

"I'll go with Mr. Magnet," said Theodore, relying firmly on the privileges of the day....

For a time they played for position, with the intentions of Mr. Magnet showing more and more starkly through the moves of the game. At last Theodore was lured down a side street by the sight of a huge dummy fish dangling outside a tackle and bait shop, and Mr. Magnet and Marjorie, already with a dreadful feeling of complicity, made a movement so rapid it seemed to her almost a bolt for the church tower. Whatever Mr. Magnet desired to say, and whatever elasticity his mind had once possessed with regard to it, there can be no doubt that it had now become so rigid as to be sayable only in that one precise position, and in the exact order he had determined upon. But when at last they got to that high serenity, Mr. Magnet was far too hot and far too much out of breath to say anything at all for a time except an almost explosive gust or so of approbation of the scenery. "Shor' breath!" he said, "win'ey stairs always—that 'fect on me—buful sceny—Suwy—like it always."

Marjorie found herself violently disposed to laugh; indeed she had never before been so near the verge of hysterics.

"It's a perfectly lovely view," she said. "No wonder you wanted me to see it."

"Naturally," said Mr. Magnet, "wanted you to see it."

Marjorie, with a skill her mother might have envied, wriggled into a half-sitting position in an embrasure and concentrated herself upon the broad wooded undulations that went about the horizon, and Mr. Magnet mopped his face with surreptitious gestures, and took deep restoring breaths.

"I've always wanted to bring you here," he said, "ever since I found it in the spring."

"It was very kind of you, Mr. Magnet," said Marjorie.

"You see," he explained, "whenever I see anything fine or rich or splendid or beautiful now, I seem to want it for you." His voice quickened as though he were repeating something that had been long in his mind. "I wish I could give you all this country. I wish I could put all that is beautiful in the world at your feet."

He watched the effect of this upon her for a moment.

"Marjorie," he said, "did you really mean what you told me the other day, that there was indeed no hope for me? I have a sort of feeling I bothered you that day, that perhaps you didn't mean all——"

He stopped short.

"I don't think I knew what I meant," said Marjorie, and Magnet gave a queer sound of relief at her words. "I don't think I know what I mean now. I don't think I can say I love you, Mr. Magnet. I would if I could. I like you very much indeed, I think you are awfully kind, you're more kind and generous than anyone I have ever known...."

Saying he was kind and generous made her through some obscure association of ideas feel that he must have understanding. She had an impulse to put her whole case before him frankly. "I wonder," she said, "if you can understand what it is to be a girl."

Then she saw the absurdity of her idea, of any such miracle of sympathy. He was entirely concentrated upon the appeal he had come prepared to make.

"Marjorie," he said, "I don't ask you to love me yet. All I ask is that you shouldn't decide not to love me."

Marjorie became aware of Theodore, hotly followed by Daffy, in the churchyard below. "I know he's up there," Theodore was manifestly saying.

Marjorie faced her lover gravely.

"Mr. Magnet," she said, "I will certainly promise you that."

"I would rather be your servant, rather live for your happiness, than do anything else in all the world," said Mr. Magnet. "If you would trust your life to me, if you would deign—." He paused to recover his thread. "If you would deign to let me make life what it should be for you, take every care from your shoulders, face every responsibility——"

Marjorie felt she had to hurry. She could almost feel the feet of Theodore coming up that tower.

"Mr. Magnet," she said, "you don't understand. You don't realize what I am. You don't know how unworthy I am—what a mere ignorant child——"

"Let me be judge of that!" cried Mr. Magnet.

They paused almost like two actors who listen for the prompter. It was only too obvious that both were aware of a little medley of imperfectly subdued noises below. Theodore had got to the ladder that made the last part of the ascent, and there Daffy had collared him. "My birthday," said Theodore. "Come down! You shan't go up there!" said Daffy. "You mustn't, Theodore!" "Why not?" There was something like a scuffle, and whispers. Then it would seem Theodore went—reluctantly and with protests. But the conflict receded.

"Marjorie!" said Mr. Magnet, as though there had been no pause, "if you would consent only to make an experiment, if you would try to love me. Suppose you tried an engagement. I do not care how long I waited...."

He paused. "Will you try?" he urged upon her distressed silence.

She felt as though she forced the word. "Yes!" she said in a very low voice.

Then it seemed to her that Mr. Magnet leapt upon her. She felt herself pulled almost roughly from the embrasure, and he had kissed her. She struggled in his embrace. "Mr. Magnet!" she said. He lifted her face and kissed her lips. "Marjorie!" he said, and she had partly released herself.

"Oh don't kiss me," she cried, "don't kiss me yet!"

"But a kiss!"

"I don't like it."

"I beg your pardon!" he said. "I forgot——. But you.... You.... I couldn't help it."

She was suddenly wildly sorry for what she had done. She felt she was going to cry, to behave absurdly.

"I want to go down," she said.

"Marjorie, you have made me the happiest of men! All my life, all my strength I will spend in showing you that you have made no mistake in trusting me——"

"Yes," she said, "yes," and wondered what she could say or do. It seemed to him that her shrinking pose was the most tenderly modest thing he had ever seen.

"Oh my dear!" he said, and restrained himself and took her passive hand and kissed it.

"I want to go down to them!" she insisted.

He paused on the topmost rungs of the ladder, looking unspeakable things at her. Then he turned to go down, and for the second time in her life she saw that incipient thinness....

"I am sure you will never be sorry," he said....

They found Mr. and Mrs. Pope in the churchyard.

Mr. Pope was reading with amusement for the third time an epitaph that had caught his fancy—

>   "Lands ever bright, days ever fair,
>   And yet we weep that he is there."

he read. "You know that's really Good. That ought to be printed somewhere."

Mrs. Pope glanced sharply at her daughter's white face, and found an enigma. Then she looked at Mr. Magnet.

There was no mistake about Mr. Magnet. Marjorie had accepted him, whatever else she had felt or done.

§ 14

Marjorie's feelings for the rest of the day are only to be accounted for on the supposition that she was overwrought. She had a preposterous reaction. She had done this thing with her eyes open after days of deliberation, and now she felt as though she was caught in a trap. The clearest thing in her mind was that Mr. Magnet had taken hold of her and kissed her, kissed her on the lips, and that presently he would do it again. And also she was asking herself with futile reiteration why she had got into debt at Oxbridge? Why she had got into debt? For such silly little things too!

Nothing definite was said in her hearing about the engagement, but everybody seemed to understand. Mr. Pope was the most demonstrative, he took occasion to rap her hard upon the back, his face crinkled with a resolute kindliness. "Ah!" he said, "Sly Maggots!"

He also administered several resounding blows to Magnet's shoulder blades, and irradiated the party with a glow of benevolent waggery. Marjorie submitted without an answer to these paternal intimations. Mrs. Pope did no more than watch her daughter. Invisible but overwhelming forces were busy in bringing Marjorie and her glowing lover alone together again. It happened at last, as he was departing; she was almost to her inflamed imagination thrust out upon him, had to take him to the gate; and there in the shadows of the trees he kissed her "good night" with passionate effusion.

"Madge," he said, "Madge!"

She made no answer. She submitted passively to his embrace, and then suddenly and dexterously disengaged herself from him, ran in, and without saying good-night to anyone went to her room to bed.

Mr. Pope was greatly amused by this departure from the customary routine of life, and noted it archly.

When Daffy came up Marjorie was ostentatiously going to sleep....

As she herself was dropping off Daffy became aware of an odd sound, somehow familiar, and yet surprising and disconcerting.

Suddenly wide awake again, she started up. Yes there was no mistake about it! And yet it was very odd.

"Madge, what's up?"

No answer.

"I say! you aren't crying, Madge, are you?"

Then after a long interval: "Madge!"

An answer came in a muffled voice, almost as if Marjorie had something in her mouth. "Oh shut it, old Daffy."

"But Madge?" said Daffy after reflection.

"Shut it. Do shut it! Leave me alone, I say! Can't you leave me alone? Oh!"—and for a moment she let her sobs have way with her—"Daffy, don't worry me. Old Daffy! Please!"

Daffy sat up for a long time in the stifled silence that ensued, and then like a sensible sister gave it up, and composed herself again to slumber....

Outside watching the window in a state of nebulous ecstasy, was Mr. Magnet, moonlit and dewy. It was a high serene night with a growing moon and a scattered company of major stars, and if no choir of nightingales sang there was at least a very active nightjar. "More than I hoped," whispered Mr. Magnet, "more than I dared to hope." He was very sleepy, but it seemed to him improper to go to bed on such a night—on such an occasion.

CHAPTER THE THIRD

The Man Who Fell Out of the Sky

§ 1

For the next week Marjorie became more nearly introspective than she had ever been in her life before. She began to doubt her hitherto unshaken conviction that she was a single, consistent human being. She found such discords and discrepancies between mood and mood, between the conviction of this hour and the feeling of that, that it seemed to her she was rather a collection of samples of emotion and attitude than anything so simple as an individual.

For example, there can be no denying there was one Marjorie in the bundle who was immensely set up by the fact that she was engaged, and going to be at no very remote date mistress of a London house. She was profoundly Plessingtonian, and quite the vulgarest of the lot. The new status she had attained and the possibly beautiful house and the probably successful dinner-parties and the arrangements and the importance of such a life was the substance of this creature's thought. She designed some queenly dresses. This was the Marjorie most in evidence when it came to talking with her mother and Daphne. I am afraid she patronized Daphne, and ignored the fact that Daphne, who had begun with a resolute magnanimity, was becoming annoyed and resentful.

And she thought of things she might buy, and the jolly feeling of putting them about and making fine effects with them. One thing she told Daphne, she had clearly resolved upon; the house should be always full and brimming over with beautiful flowers. "I've always wished mother would have more flowers—and not keep them so long when she has them...."

Another Marjorie in the confusion of her mind was doing her sincerest, narrow best to appreciate and feel grateful for and return the devotion of Mr. Magnet. This Marjorie accepted and even elaborated his views, laid stress on his voluntary subjection, harped upon his goodness, brought her to kiss him.

"I don't deserve all this love," this side of Marjorie told Magnet. "But I mean to learn to love you——"

"My dear one!" cried Magnet, and pressed her hand....

A third Marjorie among the many was an altogether acuter and less agreeable person. She was a sprite of pure criticism, and in spite of the utmost efforts to suppress her, she declared night and day in the inner confidences of Marjorie's soul that she did not believe in Mr. Magnet's old devotion at all. She was anti-Magnet, a persistent insurgent. She was dreadfully unsettling. It was surely this Marjorie that wouldn't let the fact of his baldness alone, and who discovered and insisted upon a curious unbeautiful flatness in his voice whenever he was doing his best to speak from the heart. And as for this devotion, what did it amount to? A persistent unimaginative besetting of Marjorie, a growing air of ownership, an expansive, indulgent, smiling disposition to thwart and control. And he was always touching her! Whenever he came near her she would wince at the freedoms a large, kind hand might take with her elbow or wrist, at a possible sudden, clumsy pat at some erring strand of hair.

Then there was an appraising satisfaction in his eye.

On the third day of their engagement he began, quite abruptly, to call her "Magsy." "We'll end this scandal of a Girl Pope," he said. "Magsy Magnet, you'll be—M.M. No women M.P.'s for us, Magsy...."

She became acutely critical of his intellectual quality. She listened with a new alertness to the conversations at the dinner-table, the bouts of wit with her father. She carried off utterances and witticism for maturer reflection. She was amazed to find how little they could withstand the tests and acids of her mind. So many things, such wide and interesting fields, he did not so much think about as cover with a large enveloping shallowness....

He came strolling around the vicarage into the garden one morning about eleven, though she had not expected him until lunch-time; and she was sitting with her feet tucked up on the aged but still practicable garden-seat reading Shaw's "Common Sense of Municipal Trading." He came and leant over the back of the seat, and she looked up, said "Good morning. Isn't it perfectly lovely?" and indicated by a book still open that her interest in it remained alive.

"What's the book, Magsy?" he asked, took it out of her slightly resisting hand, closed it and read the title. "Um," he said; "Isn't this a bit stiff for little women's brains?"

All the rebel Marjories were up in arms at that.

"Dreadful word, 'Municipal.' I don't like it." He shook his head with a grimace of humorous distaste.

"I suppose women have as good brains as men," said Marjorie, "if it comes to that."

"Better," said Magnet. "That's why they shouldn't trouble about horrid things like Municipal and Trading.... On a day like this!"

"Don't you think this sort of thing is interesting?"

"Oh!" he said, and flourished the book. "Come! And besides—Shaw!"

"He makes a very good case."

"But he's such a—mountebank."

"Does that matter? He isn't a mountebank there."

"He's not sincere. I doubt if you had a serious book on Municipal Trading, Magsy, whether you'd make head or tail of it. It's a stiff subject. Shaw just gets his chance for a smart thing or so.... I'd rather you read a good novel."

He really had the air of taking her reading in hand.

"You think I ought not to read an intelligent book."

"I think we ought to leave those things to the people who understand."

"But we ought to understand."

He smiled wisely. "There's a lot of things you have to understand," he said, "nearer home than this."

Marjorie was ablaze now. "What a silly thing to say!" she cried, with an undergraduate's freedom. "Really, you are talking nonsense! I read that book because it interests me. If I didn't, I should read something else. Do you mean to suggest that I'm reading like a child, who holds a book upside down?"

She was so plainly angry that he was taken aback. "I don't mean to suggest—" he began, and turned to greet the welcome presence, the interrogative eye of Mrs. Pope.

"Here we are!" he said, "having a quarrel!"

"Marjorie!" said Mrs. Pope.

"Oh, it's serious!" said Mr. Magnet, and added with a gleam: "It's about Municipal Trading!"

Mrs. Pope knew the wicked little flicker in Marjorie's eye better than Mr. Magnet. She had known it from the nursery, and yet she had never quite mastered its meaning. She had never yet realized it was Marjorie, she had always regarded it as something Marjorie, some other Marjorie, ought to keep under control. So now she adopted a pacificatory tone.

"Oh! lovers' quarrels," she said, floating over the occasion. "Lovers' quarrels. You mustn't ask me to interfere!"

Marjorie, already a little ashamed of her heat, thought for an instant she ought to stand that, and then decided abruptly with a return to choler that she would not do so. She stood up, and held out her hand for her book.

"Mr. Magnet," she said to her mother with remarkable force and freedom as she took it, "has been talking unutterable nonsense. I don't call that a lovers' quarrel—anyhow."

Then, confronted with a double astonishment, and having no more to say, she picked up her skirt quite unnecessarily, and walked with a heavenward chin indoors.

"I'm afraid," explained Mr. Magnet, "I was a little too free with one of Magsy's favourite authors."

"Which is the favourite author now?" asked Mrs. Pope, after a reflective pause, with a mother's indulgent smile.

"Shaw." He raised amused eyebrows. "It's just the age, I suppose."

"She's frightfully loyal while it lasts," said Mrs. Pope. "No one dare say a word against them."

"I think it's adorable of her," said Mr. Magnet—with an answering loyalty and gusto.

The aviation accident occurred while Mrs. Pope, her two eldest daughters, and Mr. Magnet were playing golf-croquet upon the vicarage lawn. It was a serene, hot afternoon, a little too hot to take a game seriously, and the four little figures moved slowly over the green and grouped and dispersed as the game required. Mr. Magnet was very fond of golf-croquet, he displayed a whimsical humour and much invention at this game, it was not too exacting physically; and he could make his ball jump into the air in the absurdest manner. Occasionally he won a laugh from Marjorie or Daffy. No one else was in sight; the pseudo-twins and Theodore and Toupee were in the barn, and Mr. Pope was six miles away at Wamping, lying prone, nibbling grass blades and watching a county cricket match, as every good Englishman, who knows what is expected of him, loves to do.... Click went ball and mallet, and then after a long interval, click. It seemed incredible that anything could possibly happen before tea.

But this is no longer the world it was. Suddenly this tranquil scene was slashed and rent by the sound and vision of a monoplane tearing across the heavens.

A purring and popping arrested Mr. Magnet in mid jest, and the monster came sliding up the sky over the trees beside the church to the east, already near enough to look big, a great stiff shape, big buff sails stayed with glittering wire, and with two odd little wheels beneath its body. It drove up the sky, rising with a sort of upward heaving, until the croquet players could see the driver and a passenger perched behind him quite clearly. It passed a little to the right of the church tower and only a few yards above the level of the flagstaff, there wasn't fifty feet of clearance altogether, and as it did so Marjorie could see both driver and passenger making hasty movements. It became immense and over-shadowing, and every one stood rigid as it swept across the sun above the vicarage chimneys. Then it seemed to drop twenty feet or so abruptly, and then both the men cried out as it drove straight for the line of poplars between the shrubbery and the meadow. "Oh, oh, OH!" cried Mrs. Pope and Daffy. Evidently the aviator was trying to turn sharply; the huge thing banked, but not enough, and came about and slipped away until its wing was slashing into the tree tops with a thrilling swish of leaves and the snapping of branches and stays.

"Run!" cried Magnet, and danced about the lawn, and the three ladies rushed sideways as the whole affair slouched down on them. It came on its edge, hesitated whether to turn over as a whole, then crumpled, and amidst a volley of smashing and snapping came to rest amidst ploughed-up turf, a clamorous stench of petrol, and a cloud of dust and blue smoke within twenty yards of them. The two men had jumped to clear the engine, had fallen headlong, and were now both covered by the fabric of the shattered wing.

It was all too spectacular for word or speech until the thing lay still. Even then the croquet players stood passive for awhile waiting for something to happen. It took some seconds to reconcile their minds to this sudden loss of initiative in a monster that had been so recently and threateningly full of go. It seemed quite a long time before it came into Marjorie's head that she ought perhaps to act in some way. She saw a tall young man wriggling on all fours from underneath the wreckage of fabric. He stared at her rather blankly. She went forward with a vague idea of helping him. He stood up, swayed doubtfully on his legs, turned, and became energetic, struggling mysteriously with the edge of the left wing. He gasped and turned fierce blue eyes over his shoulder.

"Help me to hold the confounded thing up!" he cried, with a touch of irritation in his voice at her attitude.

Marjorie at once seized the edge of the plane and pushed. The second man, in a peculiar button-shaped head-dress, was lying crumpled up underneath, his ear and cheek were bright with blood, and there was a streak of blood on the ground near his head.

"That's right. Can you hold it if I use only one hand?"

Marjorie gasped "Yes," with a terrific weight as it seemed suddenly on her wrists.

"Right O," and the tall young man had thrust himself backwards under the plane until it rested on his back, and collared the prostrate man. "Keep it up!" he said fiercely when Marjorie threatened to give way. He seemed to assume that she was there to obey orders, and with much grunting and effort he had dragged his companion clear of the wreckage.

The man's face was a mass of blood, and he was sickeningly inert to his companion's lugging.

"Let it go," said the tall young man, and Marjorie thanked heaven as the broken wing flapped down again.

She came helpfully to his side, and became aware of Daffy and her mother a few paces off. Magnet—it astonished her—was retreating hastily. But he had to go away because the sight of blood upset him—so much that it was always wiser for him to go away.

"Is he hurt?" cried Mrs. Pope.

"We both are," said the tall young man, and then as though these other people didn't matter and he and Marjorie were old friends, he said: "Can we turn him over?"

"I think so." Marjorie grasped the damaged man's shoulder and got him over skilfully.

"Will you get some water?" said the tall young man to Daffy and Mrs. Pope, in a way that sent Daffy off at once for a pail.

"He wants water," she said to the parlourmaid who was hurrying out of the house.

The tall young man had gone down on his knees by his companion, releasing his neck, and making a hasty first examination of his condition. "The pneumatic cap must have saved his head," he said, throwing the thing aside. "Lucky he had it. He can't be badly hurt. Just rubbed his face along the ground. Silly thing to have come as we did."

He felt the heart, and tried the flexibility of an arm.

"That's all right," he said.

He became judicial and absorbed over the problems of his friend's side. "Um," he remarked. He knelt back and regarded Marjorie for the first time. "Thundering smash," he said. His face relaxed into an agreeable smile. "He only bought it last week."

"Is he hurt?"

"Rib, I think—or two ribs perhaps. Stunned rather. All this—just his nose."

He regarded Marjorie and Marjorie him for a brief space. He became aware of Mrs. Pope on his right hand. Then at a clank behind, he turned round to see Daphne advancing with a pail of water. The two servants were now on the spot, and the odd-job man, and the old lady who did out the church, and Magnet hovered doubtfully in the distance. Suddenly with shouts and barks of sympathetic glee the pseudo-twins, Theodore and Toupee shot out of the house. New thoughts were stirring in the young aviator. He rose, wincing a little as he did so. "I'm afraid I'm a little rude," he said.

"I do hope your friend isn't hurt," said Mrs. Pope, feeling the duty of a hostess.

"He's not hurt much—so far as I can see. Haven't we made rather a mess of your lawn?"

"Oh, not at all!" said Mrs. Pope.

"We have. If that is your gardener over there, it would be nice if he kept back the people who seem to be hesitating beyond those trees. There will be more presently. I'm afraid I must throw myself on your hands." He broke into a chuckle for a moment. "I have, you know. Is it possible to get a doctor? My friend's not hurt so very much, but still he wants expert handling. He's Sir Rupert Solomonson, from"—he jerked his head back—"over beyond Tunbridge Wells. My name's Trafford."

"I'm Mrs. Pope and these are my daughters."

Trafford bowed. "We just took the thing out for a lark," he said.

Marjorie had been regarding the prostrate man. His mouth was a little open, and he showed beautiful teeth. Apart from the dry blood upon him he was not an ill-looking man. He was manifestly a Jew, a square-rigged Jew (you have remarked of course that there are square-rigged Jews, whose noses are within bounds, and fore-and-aft Jews, whose noses aren't), with not so much a bullet-head as a round-shot, cropped like the head of a Capuchin monkey. Suddenly she was down and had his head on her knee, with a quick movement that caught Trafford's eye. "He's better," she said. "His eyelids flickered. Daffy, bring the water."

She had felt a queer little repugnance at first with this helpless man, but now that professional nurse who lurks in the composition of so many women, was uppermost. "Give me your handkerchief," she said to Trafford, and with Daffy kneeling beside her and also interested, and Mrs. Pope a belated but more experienced and authoritative third, Sir Rupert was soon getting the best of attention.

"Wathall..." said Sir Rupert suddenly, and tried again: "Wathall." A third effort gave "Wathall about, eh?"

"If we could get him into the shade," said Marjorie.

"Woosh," cried Sir Rupert. "Weeeooo!"

"That's all right," said Trafford. "It's only a rib or two."

"Eeeeeyoooo!" said Sir Rupert.

"Exactly. We're going to carry you out of the glare."

"Don't touch me," said Sir Rupert. "Gooo."

It took some little persuasion before Sir Rupert would consent to be moved, and even then he was for a time—oh! crusty. But presently Trafford and the two girls had got him into the shade of a large bush close to where in a circle of rugs and cushions the tea things lay prepared. There they camped. The helpful odd-job man was ordered to stave off intruders from the village; water, towels, pillows were forthcoming. Mr. Magnet reappeared as tentative assistance, and Solomonson became articulate and brave and said he'd nothing but a stitch in his side. In his present position he wasn't at all uncomfortable. Only he didn't want any one near him. He enforced that by an appealing smile. The twins, invited to fetch the doctor, declined, proffering Theodore. They had conceived juvenile passions for the tall young man, and did not want to leave him. He certainly had a very nice face. So Theodore after walking twice round the wreckage, tore himself away and departed on Rom's bicycle. Enquiry centred on Solomonson for a time. His face, hair and neck were wet but no longer bloody, and he professed perfect comfort so long as he wasn't moved, and no one came too near him. He was very clear about that though perfectly polite, and scrutinized their faces to see if they were equally clear. Satisfied upon this point he closed his eyes and spoke no more. He looked then like a Capuchin monkey lost in pride. There came a pause. Every one was conscious of having risen to an emergency and behaved well under unusual circumstances. The young man's eye rested on the adjacent tea-things, lacking nothing but the coronation of the teapot.

"Why not," he remarked, "have tea?"

"If you think your friend——" began Mrs. Pope.

"Oh! he's all right. Aren't you, Solomonson? There's nothing more now until the doctor."

"Only want to be left alone," said Solomonson, and closed his heavy eyelids again.

Mrs. Pope told the maids, with an air of dismissal, to get tea.

"We can keep an eye on him," said Trafford.

Marjorie surveyed her first patient with a pretty unconscious mixture of maternal gravity and girlish interest, and the twins to avoid too openly gloating upon the good looks of Trafford, chose places and secured cushions round the tea-things, calculating to the best of their ability how they might secure the closest proximity to him. Mr. Magnet and Toupee had gone to stare at the monoplane; they were presently joined by the odd-job man in an interrogative mood. "Pretty complete smash, sir!" said the odd-job man, and then perceiving heads over the hedge by the churchyard, turned back to his duty of sentinel. Daffy thought of the need of more cups and plates and went in to get them, and Mrs. Pope remarked that she did hope Sir Rupert was not badly hurt....

"Extraordinary all this is," remarked Mr. Trafford. "Now, here we were after lunch, twenty miles away—smoking cigars and with no more idea of having tea with you than—I was going to say—flying. But that's out of date now. Then we just thought we'd try the thing.... Like a dream."

He addressed himself to Marjorie: "I never feel that life is quite real until about three days after things have happened. Never. Two hours ago I had not the slightest intention of ever flying again."

"But haven't you flown before?" asked Mrs. Pope.

"Not much. I did a little at Sheppey, but it's so hard for a poor man to get his hands on a machine. And here was Solomonson, with this thing in his hangar, eating its head off. Let's take it out," I said, "and go once round the park. And here we are.... I thought it wasn't wise for him to come...."

Sir Rupert, without opening his eyes, was understood to assent.

"Do you know," said Trafford, "The sight of your tea makes me feel frightfully hungry."

"I don't think the engine's damaged?" he said cheerfully, "do you?" as Magnet joined them. "The ailerons are in splinters, and the left wing's not much better. But that's about all except the wheels. One falls so much lighter than you might suppose—from the smash.... Lucky it didn't turn over. Then, you know, the engine comes on the top of you, and you're done."

§ 3

The doctor arrived after tea, with a bag and a stethoscope in a small coffin-like box, and the Popes and Mr. Magnet withdrew while Sir Rupert was carefully sounded, tested, scrutinized, questioned, watched and examined in every way known to medical science. The outcome of the conference was presently communicated to the Popes by Mr. Trafford and the doctor. Sir Rupert was not very seriously injured, but he was suffering from concussion and shock, two of his ribs were broken and his wrist sprained, unless perhaps one of the small bones was displaced. He ought to be bandaged up and put to bed....

"Couldn't we—" said Mrs. Pope, but the doctor assured her his own house was quite the best place. There Sir Rupert could stay for some days. At present the cross-country journey over the Downs or by the South Eastern Railway would be needlessly trying and painful. He would with the Popes' permission lie quietly where he was for an hour or so, and then the doctor would come with a couple of men and a carrying bed he had, and take him off to his own house. There he would be, as Mr. Trafford said, "as right as ninepence," and Mr. Trafford could put up either at the Red Lion with Mr. Magnet or in the little cottage next door to the doctor. (Mr. Trafford elected for the latter as closer to his friend.) As for the smashed aeroplane, telegrams would be sent at once to Sir Rupert's engineers at Chesilbury, and they would have all that cleared away by mid-day to-morrow....

The doctor departed; Sir Rupert, after stimulants, closed his eyes, and Mr. Trafford seated himself at the tea-things for some more cake, as though introduction by aeroplane was the most regular thing in the world.

He had very pleasant and easy manners, an entire absence of self-consciousness, and a quick talkative disposition that made him very rapidly at home with everybody. He described all the sensations of flight, his early lessons and experiments, and in the utmost detail the events of the afternoon that had led to this disastrous adventure. He made his suggestion of "trying the thing" seem the most natural impulse in the world. The bulk of the conversation fell on him; Mr. Magnet, save for the intervention of one or two jests, was quietly observant; the rest were well disposed to listen. And as Mr.

Trafford talked his eye rested ever and again on Marjorie with the faintest touch of scrutiny and perplexity, and she, too, found a curious little persuasion growing up in her mind that somewhere, somehow, she and he had met and had talked rather earnestly. But how and where eluded her altogether....

They had sat for an hour—the men from the doctor's seemed never coming—when Mr. Pope returned unexpectedly from his cricket match, which had ended a little prematurely in a rot on an over-dry wicket. He was full of particulars of the day's play, and how Wiper had got a most amazing catch and held it, though he fell; how Jenks had deliberately bowled at a man's head, he believed, and little Gibbs thrown a man out from slip. He was burning to tell all this in the utmost detail to Magnet and his family, so that they might at least share the retrospect of his pleasure. He had thought out rather a good pun on Wiper, and he was naturally a little thwarted to find all this good, rich talk crowded out by a more engrossing topic.

At the sight of a stranger grouped in a popular manner beside the tea-things, he displayed a slight acerbity, which was if anything increased by the discovery of a prostrate person with large brown eyes and an expression of Oriental patience and disdain, in the shade of a bush near by. At first he seemed scarcely to grasp Mrs. Pope's explanations, and regarded Sir Rupert with an expression that bordered on malevolence. Then, when his attention was directed to the smashed machine upon the lawn, he broke out into a loud indignant: "Good God! What next?"

He walked towards the wreckage, disregarding Mr. Trafford beside him. "A man can't go away from his house for an hour!" he complained.

"I can assure you we did all we could to prevent it," said Trafford.

"Ought never to have had it to prevent," said Mr. Pope. "Is your friend hurt?"

"A rib—and shock," said Trafford.

"Well—he deserves it," said Mr. Pope. "Rather than launch myself into the air in one of those infernal things, I'd be stood against a wall and shot."

"Tastes differ, of course," said Trafford, with unruffled urbanity.

"You'll have all this cleared away," said Mr. Pope.

"Mechanics—oh! a complete break-down party—are speeding to us in fast motors," said Trafford. "Thanks to the kindness of your domestic in taking a telegram for me."

"Hope they won't kill any one," said Mr. Pope, and just for a moment the conversation hung fire. "And your friend?" he asked.

"He goes in the next ten minutes—well, whenever the litter comes from the doctor's. Poor old Solomonson!"

"Solomonson?"

"Sir Rupert."

"Oh!" said Mr. Pope. "Is that the Pigmentation Solomonson?"

"I believe he does do some beastly company of that sort," said Trafford. "Isn't it amazing we didn't smash our engine?"

Sir Rupert Solomonson was indeed a familiar name to Mr. Pope. He had organized the exploitation of a number of pigment and bye-product patents, and the ordinary and deferred shares of his syndicate has risen to so high a price as to fill Mr. Pope with the utmost confidence in their future; indeed he had bought considerably, withdrawing capital to do so from an Argentine railway whose stock had awakened his distaste and a sort of moral aversion by slumping heavily after a bad wheat and linseed harvest. This discovery did much to mitigate his first asperity, his next remark to Trafford was almost neutral, and he was even asking Sir Rupert whether he could do anything to make him comfortable, when the doctor returned with a litter, borne by four hastily compiled bearers.

§ 4

Some brightness seemed to vanish when the buoyant Mr. Trafford, still undauntedly cheerful, limped off after his more injured friend, and disappeared through the gate. Marjorie found herself in a world whose remaining manhood declined to see anything but extreme annoyance in this gay, exciting rupture of the afternoon. "Good God!" said Mr. Pope. "What next? What next?"

"Registration, I hope," said Mr. Magnet,—"and

relegation to the desert of Sahara."

"One good thing about it," said Mr. Pope—"it all wastes petrol. And when the petrol supply gives out—they're done."

"Certainly we might all have been killed!" said Mrs. Pope, feeling she had to bear her witness against their visitors, and added: "If we hadn't moved out of the way, that is."

There was a simultaneous movement towards the shattered apparatus, about which a small contingent of villagers, who had availed themselves of the withdrawal of the sentinel, had now assembled.

"Look at it!" said Mr. Pope, with bitter hostility. "Look at it!"

Everyone had anticipated his command.

"They'll never come to anything," said Mr. Pope, after a pause of silent hatred.

"But they have to come to something," said Marjorie.

"They've come to smash!" said Mr. Magnet, with the true humorist's air.

"But consider the impudence of this invasion, the wild—objectionableness of it!"

"They're nasty things," said Mr. Magnet. "Nasty things!"

A curious spirit of opposition stirred in Marjorie. It seemed to her that men who play golf-croquet and watch cricket matches have no business to contemn men who risk their lives in the air. She sought for some controversial opening.

"Isn't the engine rather wonderful?" she remarked.

Mr. Magnet regarded the engine with his head a little on one side. "It's the usual sort," he said.

"There weren't engines like that twenty years ago."

"There weren't people like you twenty years

ago," said Mr. Magnet, smiling wisely and kindly, and turned his back on the thing.

Mr. Pope followed suit. He was filled with the bitter thought that he would never now be able to tell the history of the remarkable match he had witnessed. It was all spoilt for him—spoilt for ever. Everything was disturbed and put out.

"They've left us our tennis lawn," he said, with a not unnatural resentment passing to invitation. "What do you say, Magnet? Now you've begun the game you must keep it up?"

"If Marjorie, or Mrs. Pope, or Daffy...?" said Magnet.

Mrs. Pope declared the house required her. And so with the gravest apprehensions, and an insincere compliment to their father's energy, Daffy and Marjorie made up a foursome for that healthy and invigorating game. But that evening Mr. Pope got his serve well into the bay of the sagging net almost at once, and with Marjorie in the background taking anything he left her, he won quite easily, and everything became pleasant again. Magnet gloated upon Marjorie and served her like a missionary giving Bibles to heathen children, he seemed always looking at her instead of the ball, and except for a slight disposition on the part of Daffy to slash, nothing could have been more delightful. And at supper Mr. Pope, rather crushing his wife's attempt to recapitulate the more characteristic sayings and doings of Sir Rupert and his friend, did after all succeed in giving every one a very good idea indeed of the more remarkable incidents of the cricket match at Wamping, and made the pun he had been accustomed to use upon the name of Wiper in a new and improved form. A general talk about cricket and the Immense Good of cricket followed. Mr. Pope said he would make cricket-playing compulsory for every English boy.

Everyone it seemed to Marjorie was forgetting that dark shape athwart the lawn, and all the immense implication of its presence, with a deliberate and irrational skill, and she noted that the usual move towards the garden at the end of the evening was not made.

§ 5

In the night time Marjorie had a dream that she was flying about in the world on a monoplane with Mr. Trafford as a passenger.

Then Mr. Trafford disappeared, and she was flying about alone with a curious uneasy feeling that in a minute or so she would be unable any longer to manage the machine.

Then her father and Mr. Magnet appeared very far below, walking about and disapproving of her. Mr. Magnet was shaking his head very, very sagely, and saying: "Rather a stiff job for little Marjorie," and her father was saying she would be steadier when she married. And then, she wasn't clear how, the engine refused to work until her bills were paid, and she began to fall, and fall, and fall towards Mr. Magnet. She tried frantically to pay her bills. She was falling down the fronts of skyscrapers and precipices—and Mr. Magnet was waiting for her below with a quiet kindly smile that grew wider and wider and wider....

She woke up palpitating.

§ 6

Next morning a curious restlessness came upon Marjorie. Conceivably it was due to the absence of Magnet, who had gone to London to deliver his long promised address on The Characteristics of English Humour to the Literati Club. Conceivably she missed his attentions. But it crystallized out in the early afternoon into the oddest form, a powerful craving to go to the little town of Pensting, five miles off, on the other side of Buryhamstreet, to buy silk shoelaces.

She decided to go in the donkey cart. She communicated her intention to her mother, but she did not communicate an equally definite intention to be reminded suddenly of Sir Rupert Solomonson as she was passing the surgery, and make an inquiry on the spur of the moment—it wouldn't surely be anything but a kindly and justifiable impulse to do that. She might see Mr. Trafford perhaps, but there was no particular harm in that.

It is also to be remarked that finding Theodore a little disposed to encumber her vehicle with his presence she expressed her delight at being released from the need of going, and abandoned the whole expedition to him—knowing as she did perfectly well that if Theodore hated anything more than navigating the donkey cart alone, it was going unprotected into a shop to buy articles of feminine apparel—until he chucked the whole project and went fishing—if one can call it fishing when there are no fish and the fisherman knows it—in the decadent ornamental water.

And it is also to be remarked that as Marjorie approached the surgery she was seized with an absurd and powerful shyness, so that not only did she not call at the surgery, she did not even look at the surgery, she gazed almost rigidly straight ahead, telling herself, however, that she merely deferred that kindly impulse until she had bought her laces. And so it happened that about half a mile beyond the end of Buryhamstreet she came round a corner upon Trafford, and by a singular fatality he also was driving a donkey, or, rather, was tracing a fan-like pattern on the road with a donkey's hoofs. It was a very similar donkey to Marjorie's, but the vehicle was a governess cart, and much smarter than Marjorie's turn-out. His ingenuous face displayed great animation at the sight of her, and as she drew alongside he hailed her with an almost unnatural ease of manner.

"Hullo!" he cried. "I'm taking the air. You seem to be able to drive donkeys forward. How do you do it? I can't. Never done anything so dangerous in my life before. I've just been missed by two motor cars, and hung for a terrible minute with my left wheel on the very verge of an unfathomable ditch. I could hear the little ducklings far, far below, and bits of mould dropping. I tried to count before the splash. Aren't you—white?"

"But why are you doing it?"

"One must do something. I'm bandaged up and can't walk. It hurt my leg more than I knew—your doctor says. Solomonson won't talk of anything but how he feels, and I don't care a rap how he feels. So I got this thing and came out with it."

Marjorie made her inquiries. There came a little pause.

"Some day no one will believe that men were ever so foolish as to trust themselves to draught animals," he remarked. "Hullo! Look out! The horror of it!"

A large oil van—a huge drum on wheels—motor-driven, had come round the corner, and after a preliminary and quite insufficient hoot, bore down upon them, and missing Trafford as it seemed by a miracle, swept past. Both drivers did wonderful things with whips and reins, and found themselves alone in the road again, with their wheels locked and an indefinite future.

"I leave the situation to you," said Trafford. "Or shall we just sit and talk until the next motor car kills us?"

"We ought to make an effort," said Marjorie, cheerfully, and descended to lead the two beasts.

Assisted by an elderly hedger, who had been taking a disregarded interest in them for some time, she separated the wheels and got the two donkeys abreast. The old hedger's opinion of their safety on the king's highway was expressed by his action rather than his words; he directed the beasts towards a shady lane that opened at right angles to the road. He stood by their bridles while Marjorie resumed her seat.

"It seems to me clearly a case for compromise," said Trafford. "You want to go that way, I want to go that way. Let us both go this way. It is by such arrangements that civilization becomes possible."

He dismissed the hedger generously and resumed his reins.

"Shall we race?" he asked.

"With your leg?" she inquired.

"No; with the donkeys. I say, this is rather a lark. At first I thought it was both dangerous and dull. But things have changed. I am in beastly high spirits. I feel there will be a cry before night; but still, I am——I wanted the companionship of an unbroken person. It's so jolly to meet you again."

"Again?"

"After the year before last."

"After the year before last?"

"You didn't know," said Trafford, "I had met you before? How aggressive I must have seemed! Well, I wasn't quite clear. I spent the greater part of last night—my ankle being foolish in the small hours—in trying to remember how and where."

"I don't remember," said Marjorie.

"I remembered you very distinctly, and some things I thought about you, but not where it had happened. Then in the night I got it. It is a puzzle, isn't it? You see, I was wearing a black gown, and I had been out of the sunlight for some months—and my eye, I remember it acutely, was bandaged. I'm usually bandaged somewhere.

> 'I was a King in Babylon
> And you were a Christian slave'

—I mean a candidate."

Marjorie remembered suddenly. "You're Professor Trafford."

"Not in this atmosphere. But I am at the Romeike College. And as soon as I recalled examining you I remembered it—minutely. You were intelligent, though unsound—about cryo-hydrates it was. Ah, you remember me now. As most young women are correct by rote and unintelligent in such questions, and as it doesn't matter a rap about anything of that sort, whether you are correct or not, as long as the mental gesture is right——" He paused for a moment, as though tired of his sentence. "I remembered you."

He proceeded in his easy and detached manner, that seemed to make every topic possible, to tell her his first impressions of her, and show how very distinctly indeed he remembered her.

"You set me philosophizing. I'd never examined a girls' school before, and I was suddenly struck by the spectacle of the fifty of you. What's going to become of them all?"

"I thought," he went on, "how bright you were, and how keen and eager you were—you, I mean, in particular—and just how certain it was your brightness and eagerness would be swallowed up by some silly ordinariness or other—stuffy marriage or stuffy domestic duties. The old, old story—done over again with a sort of threadbare badness. (Nothing to say against it if it's done well.) I got quite sentimental and pathetic about life's breach of faith with women. Odd, isn't it, how one's mind runs on. But that's what I thought. It's all come back to me."

Marjorie's bright, clear eye came round to him. "I don't see very much wrong with the lot of women," she reflected. "Things are different nowadays. Anyhow——"

She paused.

"You don't want to be a man?"

"No!"

She was emphatic.

"Some of us cut more sharply at life than you think," he said, plumbing her unspoken sense.

She had never met a man before who understood just how a girl can feel the slow obtuseness of his sex. It was almost as if he had found her out at something.

"Oh," she said, "perhaps you do," and looked at him with an increased interest.

"I'm half-feminine, I believe," he said. "For instance, I've got just a woman's joy in textures and little significant shapes. I know how you feel about that. I can spend hours, even now, in crystal gazing—I don't mean to see some silly revelation of some silly person's proceedings somewhere, but just for the things themselves. I wonder if you have ever been in the Natural History Museum at South Kensington, and looked at Ruskin's crystal collection? I saw it when I was a boy, and it became—I can't help the word—an obsession. The inclusions like moss and like trees, and all sorts of fantastic things, and the cleavages and enclosures with little bubbles, and the lights and shimmer—What were we talking about? Oh, about the keen way your feminine perceptions cut into things. And yet somehow I was throwing contempt on the feminine intelligence. I don't do justice to the order of my thoughts. Never mind. We've lost the thread. But I wish you knew my mother."

He went on while Marjorie was still considering the proper response to this.

"You see, I'm her only son and she brought me up, and we know each other—oh! very well. She helps with my work. She understands nearly all of it. She makes suggestions. And to this day I don't know if she's the most original or the most parasitic of creatures. And that's the way with all women and girls, it seems to me. You're as critical as light, and as undiscriminating.... I say, do I strike you as talking nonsense?"

"Not a bit," said Marjorie. "But you do go rather fast."

"I know," he admitted. "But somehow you excite me. I've been with Solomonson a week, and he's dull at all times. It was that made me take out that monoplane of his. But it did him no good."

He paused.

"They told me after the exam.," said Marjorie, "you knew more about crystallography—than anyone."

"Does that strike you as a dull subject?"

"No," said Marjorie, in a tone that invited justifications.

"It isn't. I think—naturally, that the world one goes into when one studies molecular physics is quite the most beautiful of Wonderlands.... I can assure you I work sometimes like a man who is exploring a magic palace.... Do you know anything of molecular physics?"

"You examined me," said Marjorie.

"The sense one has of exquisite and wonderful rhythms—just beyond sound and sight! And there's a taunting suggestion of its being all there, displayed and confessed, if only one were quick enough to see it. Why, for instance, when you change the composition of a felspar almost imperceptibly, do the angles change? What's the correspondence between the altered angle and the substituted atom? Why does this bit of clear stuff swing the ray of light so much out of its path, and that swing it more? Then what happens when crystals gutter down, and go into solution. The endless launching of innumerable little craft. Think what a clear solution must be if only one had ultra-microscopic eyes and could see into it, see the extraordinary patternings, the swimming circling constellations. And then the path of a ray of polarized light beating through it! It takes me like music. Do you know anything of the effects of polarized light, the sight of a slice of olivine-gabbro for instance between crossed Nicols?"

"I've seen some rock sections," said Marjorie. "I forget the names of the rocks."

"The colours?"

"Oh yes, the colours."

"Is there anything else so rich and beautiful in all the world? And every different mineral and every variety of that mineral has a different palette of colours, a different scheme of harmonies—and is telling you something."

"If only you understood."

"Exactly. All the ordinary stuff of life—you know—the carts and motor cars and dusty roads and—cinder sifting, seems so blank to me—with that persuasion of swing and subtlety beneath it all. As if the whole world was fire and crystal and aquiver—with some sort of cotton wrappers thrown over it...."

"Dust sheets," said Marjorie. "I know."

"Or like a diamond painted over!"

"With that sort of grey paint, very full of body—that lasts."

"Yes." He smiled at her. "I can't help apologetics. Most people think a professor of science is just——"

"A professor of science."

"Yes. Something all pedantries and phrases. I want to clear my character. As though it is foolish to follow a vortex ring into a vacuum, and wise to whack at a dirty golf ball on a suburban railway bank. Oh, their golf! Under high heaven!... You don't play golf, do you, by any chance?"

"Only the woman's part," said Marjorie.

"And they despise us," he said. "Solomonson can hardly hide how he despises us. Nothing is more wonderful than the way these people go on despising us who do research, who have this fever of curiosity, who won't be content with—what did you call those wrappers?"

"Dust sheets."

"Yes, dust sheets. What a life! Swaddling bands, dust sheets and a shroud! You know, research and discovery aren't nearly so difficult as people think—if only you have the courage to say a thing or try a thing now and then that it isn't usual to say or try. And after all——" he went off at a tangent, "these confounded ordinary people aren't justified in their contempt. We keep on throwing them things over our shoulders, electric bells, telephones, Marconigrams. Look at the beautiful electric trains that come towering down the

London streets at nightfall, ships of light in full sail! Twenty years ago they were as impossible as immortality. We conquer the seas for these—golfers, puts arms in their hands that will certainly blow them all to bits if ever the idiots go to war with them, come sailing out of the air on them——"

He caught Marjorie's eye and stopped.

"Falling out of the air on them," corrected Marjorie very softly.

"That was only an accident," said Mr. Trafford....

So they began a conversation in the lane where the trees met overhead that went on and went on like a devious path in a shady wood, and touched upon all manner of things....

§ 7

In the end quite a number of people were aggrieved by this dialogue, in the lane that led nowhither....

Sir Rupert Solomonson was the first to complain. Trafford had been away "three mortal hours." No one had come near him, not a soul, and there hadn't been even a passing car to cheer his ear.

Sir Rupert admitted he had to be quiet. "But not so damned quiet."

"I'd have been glad," said Sir Rupert, "if a hen had laid an egg and clucked a bit. You might have thought there had been a Resurrection or somethin', and cleared off everybody. Lord! it was deadly. I'd have sung out myself if it hadn't been for these infernal ribs...."

Mrs. Pope came upon the affair quite by accident.

"Well, Marjorie," she said as she poured tea for the family, "did you get your laces?"

"Never got there, Mummy," said Marjorie, and paused fatally.

"Didn't get there!" said Mrs. Pope. "That's worse than Theodore! Wouldn't the donkey go, poor dear?"

There was nothing to colour about, and yet Marjorie felt the warm flow in neck and cheek and brow. She threw extraordinary quantities of candour into her manner. "I had a romantic adventure," she said rather quietly. "I was going to tell you."

(Sensation.)

"You see it was like this," said Marjorie. "I ran against Mr. Trafford...."

She drank tea, and pulled herself together for a lively description of the wheel-locking and the subsequent conversation, a bright ridiculous account which made the affair happen by implication on the high road and not in a byeway, and was adorned with every facetious ornament that seemed likely to get a laugh from the children. But she talked rather fast, and she felt she forced the fun a little. However, it amused the children all right, and Theodore created a diversion by choking with his tea. From first to last Marjorie was extremely careful to avoid the affectionate scrutiny of her mother's eye. And had this lasted the whole afternoon? asked Mrs. Pope. "Oh, they'd talked for half-an-hour," said Marjorie, or more, and had driven back very slowly together. "He did all the talking. You saw what he was yesterday. And the donkeys seemed too happy together to tear them away."

"But what was it all about?" asked Daffy curious.

"He asked after you, Daffy, most affectionately," said Marjorie, and added, "several times." (Though Trafford had as a matter of fact displayed a quite remarkable disregard of all her family.)

"And," she went on, getting a plausible idea at last, "he explained all about aeroplanes. And all that sort of thing. Has Daddy gone to Wamping for some more cricket?..."

(But none of this was lost on Mrs. Pope.)

§ 8

Mr. Magnet's return next day was heralded by nearly two-thirds of a column in the Times.

The Lecture on the Characteristics of Humour had evidently been quite a serious affair, and a very imposing list of humorists and of prominent people associated with their industry had accepted the hospitality of the Literati.

Marjorie ran her eyes over the Chairman's flattering introduction, then with a queer faint flavour of hostility she reached her destined husband's utterance. She seemed to hear the flat full tones of his voice as she read, and automatically the desiccated sentences of the reporter filled out again into those rich quietly deliberate unfoldings of sound that were already too familiar to her ear.

Mr. Magnet had begun with modest disavowals. "There was a story, he said,"—so the report began—"whose hallowed antiquity ought to protect it from further exploitation, but he was tempted to repeat it because it offered certain analogies to the present situation. There were three characters in the story, a bluebottle and two Scotsmen. (Laughter.) The bluebottle buzzed on the pane, otherwise a profound silence reigned. This was broken by one of the Scotsmen trying to locate the bluebottle with zoölogical exactitude. Said this Scotsman: 'Sandy, I am thinking if yon fly is a birdie or a beastie.' The other replied: 'Man, don't spoil good whiskey with religious conversation.' (Laughter.) He was tempted, Mr. Magnet resumed, to ask himself and them why it was that they should spoil the aftereffects of a most excellent and admirably served dinner by an academic discussion on British humour. At first he was pained by the thought that they proposed to temper their hospitality with a demand for a speech. A closer inspection showed that he was to introduce a debate and that others were to speak, and that was a new element in their hospitality. Further, he was permitted to choose the subject so that he could bring their speeches within the range of his comprehension. (Laughter.) His was an easy task. He could make it easier; the best thing to do would be to say nothing at all. (Laughter.)"

For a space the reporter seemed to have omitted largely—perhaps he was changing places with his relief—and the next sentence showed Mr. Magnet engaged as it were in revising a hortus siccus of jokes. "There was the humour of facts and situations," he was saying, "or that humour of expression for which there was no human responsibility, as in the case of Irish humour; he spoke of the humour of the soil which found its noblest utterance in the bull. Humour depended largely on contrast. There was a humour of form and expression which had many local varieties. American humour had been characterized by exaggeration, the suppression of some link in the chain of argument or narrative, and a wealth of simile and metaphor which had been justly defined as the poetry of a pioneer race."...

Marjorie's attention slipped its anchor, and caught lower down upon: "In England there was a near kinship between laughter and tears; their mental relations were as close as their physical. Abroad this did not appear to be the case. It was different in France. But perhaps on the whole it would be better to leave the humour of France and what some people still unhappily chose to regard as matters open to controversy—he referred to choice of subject—out of their discussion altogether. ('Hear, hear,' and cheers.)"...

Attention wandered again. Then she remarked:—it reminded her in some mysterious way of a dropped hairpin—"It was noticeable that the pun to a great extent had become démodé...."

At this point the flight of Marjorie's eyes down the column was arrested by her father's hand gently but firmly taking possession of the Times. She yielded it without reluctance, turned to the breakfast table, and never resumed her study of the social relaxations of humorists....

Indeed she forgot it. Her mind was in a state of extreme perplexity. She didn't know what to make of herself or anything or anybody. Her mind was full of Trafford and all that he had said and done and all that he might have said and done, and it was entirely characteristic that she could not think of Magnet in any way at all except as a bar-like shadow that lay across all her memories and all the bright possibilities of this engaging person.

She thought particularly of the mobile animation of his face, the keen flash of enthusiasm in his thoughts and expressions....

It was perhaps more characteristic of her time than of her that she did not think she was dealing so much with a moral problem as an embarrassment, and that she hadn't as yet felt the first stirrings of self-reproach for the series of disingenuous proceedings that had rendered the yesterday's encounter possible. But she was restless, wildly restless as a bird whose nest is taken. She could abide nowhere. She fretted through the morning, avoided Daffy in a marked manner, and inflicted a stinging and only partially merited rebuke upon Theodore for slouching, humping and—of all trite grievances!—not washing behind his ears. As if any chap washed behind his ears! She thought tennis with the pseudo-twins might assuage her, but she broke off after losing two sets; and then she went into the garden to get fresh flowers, and picked a large bunch and left them on the piano until her mother reminded her of them. She tried a little Shaw. She struggled with an insane wish to walk through the wood behind the village and have an accidental meeting with someone who couldn't possibly appear but whom it would be quite adorable to meet. Anyhow she conquered that.

She had a curious and rather morbid indisposition to go after lunch to the station and meet Mr. Magnet as her mother wished her to do, in order to bring him straight to the vicarage to early tea, but here again reason prevailed and she went.

Mr. Magnet arrived by the 2.27, and to Marjorie's eye his alighting presence had an effect of being not so much covered with laurels as distended by them. His face seemed whiter and larger than ever. He waved a great handful of newspapers.

"Hullo, Magsy!" he said. "They've given me a thumping Press. I'm nearer swelled head than I've ever been, so mind how you touch me!"

"We'll take it down at croquet," said Marjorie.

"They've cleared that thing away?"

"And made up the lawn like a billiard table," she said.

"That makes for skill," he said waggishly. "I shall save my head after all."

For a moment he seemed to loom towards kissing her, but she averted this danger by a business-like concern for his bag. He entrusted this to a porter, and reverted to the triumph of overnight so soon as they were clear of the station. He was overflowing with kindliness towards his fellow humorists, who had appeared in force and very generously at the banquet, and had said the most charming things—some of which were in one report and some in another, and some the reporters had missed altogether—some of the kindliest.

"It's a pleasant feeling to think that a lot of good fellows think you are a good fellow," said Mr. Magnet.

He became solicitous for her. How had she got on while he was away? She asked him how one was likely to get on at Buryhamstreet; monoplanes didn't fall every day, and as she said that it occurred to her she was behaving meanly. But he was going on to his next topic before she could qualify.

"I've got something in my pocket," he remarked, and playfully: "Guess."

She did, but she wouldn't. She had a curious sinking of the heart.

"I want you to see it before anyone else," he said. "Then if you don't like it, it can go back. It's a sapphire."

He was feeling nervously in his pockets and then the little box was in her hand.

She hesitated to open it. It made everything so dreadfully concrete. And this time the sense of meanness was altogether acuter. He'd bought this in London; he'd brought it down, hoping for her approval. Yes, it was—horrid. But what was she to do?

"It's—awfully pretty," she said with the glittering symbol in her hand, and indeed he had gone to one of those artistic women who are reviving and improving upon the rich old Roman designs. "It's so beautifully made."

"I'm so glad you like it. You really do like it?"

"I don't deserve it."

"Oh! But you do like it?"

"Enormously."

"Ah! I spent an hour in choosing it."

She could see him. She felt as though she had picked his pocket.

"Only I don't deserve it, Mr. Magnet. Indeed I don't. I feel I am taking it on false pretences."

"Nonsense, Magsy. Nonsense! Slip it on your finger, girl."

"But I don't," she insisted.

He took the box from her, pocketed it and seized her hand. She drew it away from him.

"No!" she said. "I feel like a cheat. You know, I don't—I'm sure I don't love——"

"I'll love enough for two," he said, and got her hand again. "No!" he said at her gesture, "you'll wear it. Why shouldn't you?"

And so Marjorie came back along the vicarage avenue with his ring upon her hand. And Mr. Pope was evidently very glad to see him....

The family was still seated at tea upon rugs and wraps, and still discussing humorists at play, when Professor Trafford appeared, leaning on a large stick and limping, but resolute, by the church gate. "Pish!" said Mr. Pope. Marjorie tried not to reveal a certain dismay, there was dumb, rich approval in Daphne's eyes, and the pleasure of Theodore and the pseudo-twins was only too scandalously evident. "Hoo-Ray!" said Theodore, with ill-concealed relief.

Mrs. Pope was the incarnate invocation of tact as Trafford drew near.

"I hope," he said, with obvious insincerity, "I don't invade you. But Solomonson is frightfully concerned and anxious about your lawn, and whether his men cleared it up properly and put things right." His eye went about the party and rested on Marjorie. "How are you?" he said, in a friendly voice.

"Well, we seem to have got our croquet lawn back," said Mr. Pope. "And our nerves are recovering. How is Sir Rupert?"

"A little fractious," said Trafford, with the ghost of a smile.

"You'll take some tea?" said Mrs. Pope in the pause that followed.

"Thank you," said Trafford and sat down instantly.

"I saw your jolly address in the Standard," he said to Magnet. "I haven't read anything so amusing for some time."

"Rom dear," said Mrs. Pope, "will you take the pot in and get some fresh tea?"

Mr. Trafford addressed himself to the flattery of Magnet with considerable skill. He had detected a lurking hostility in the eyes of the two gentlemen that counselled him to propitiate them if he meant to maintain his footing in the vicarage, and now he talked to them almost exclusively and ignored the ladies modestly but politely in the way that seems natural and proper in a British middle-class house of the better sort. But as he talked chiefly of the improvement of motor machinery that had recently been shown at the Engineering Exhibition, he did not make that headway with Marjorie's father that he had perhaps anticipated. Mr. Pope fumed quietly for a time, and then suddenly spoke out.

"I'm no lover of machines," he said abruptly, slashing across Mr. Trafford's description.

"All our troubles began with villainous saltpetre. I'm an old-fashioned man with a nose—and a neck, and I don't want the one offended or the other broken. No, don't ask me to be interested in your valves and cylinders. What do you say, Magnet? It starts machinery in my head to hear about them...."

On such occasions as this when Mr. Pope spoke out, his horror of an anti-climax or any sort of contradiction was apt to bring the utterance to a culmination not always to be distinguished from a flight. And now he rose to his feet as he delivered himself.

"Who's for a game of tennis?" he said, "in this last uncontaminated patch of air? I and Marjorie will give you a match, Daffy—if Magnet isn't too tired to join you."

Daffy looked at Marjorie for an instant.

"We'll want you, Theodore, to look after the balls in the potatoes," said Mr. Pope lest that ingenuous mind should be corrupted behind his back....

Mrs. Pope found herself left to entertain a slightly disgruntled Trafford. Rom and Syd hovered on the off chance of notice, at the corner of the croquet lawn nearest the tea things. Mrs. Pope had already determined to make certain little matters clearer than they appeared to be to this agreeable but superfluous person, and she was greatly assisted by his opening upon the subject of her daughters. "Jolly tennis looks," he said.

"Don't they?" said Mrs. Pope. "I think it is such a graceful game for a girl."

Mr. Trafford glanced at Mrs. Pope's face, but her expression was impenetrable.

"They both like it and play it so well," she said. "Their father is so skillful and interested in games. Marjorie tells me you were her examiner a year or so ago."

"Yes. She struck my memory—her work stood out."

"Of course she is clever," said Mrs. Pope. "Or we shouldn't have sent her to Oxbridge. There she's doing quite well—quite well. Everyone says so. I don't know, of course, if Mr. Magnet will let her finish there."

"Mr. Magnet?"

"She's just engaged to him. Of course she's frightfully excited about it, and naturally he wants her to come away and marry. There's very little excuse for a long engagement.

No."

Her voice died in a musical little note, and she seemed to be scrutizing the tennis with an absorbed interest. "They've got new balls," she said, as if to herself.

Trafford had rolled over, and she fancied she detected a change in his voice when it came. "Isn't it rather a waste not to finish a university career?" he said.

"Oh, it wouldn't be wasted. Of course a girl like that will be hand and glove with her husband. She'll be able to help him with the scientific side of his jokes and all that. I sometimes wish it had been Daffy who had gone to college though. I sometimes think we've sacrificed Daffy a little. She's not the bright quickness of Marjorie, but there's something quietly solid about her mind—something stable. Perhaps I didn't want her to go away from me.... Mr. Magnet is doing wonders at the net. He's just begun to play—to please Marjorie. Don't you think he's a dreadfully amusing man, Mr. Trafford? He says such quiet things."

§ 9

The effect of this éclaircissement upon Mr. Trafford was not what it should have been. Properly he ought to have realized at once that Marjorie was for ever beyond his aspirations, and if he found it too difficult to regard her with equanimity, then he ought to have shunned her presence. But instead, after his first shock of incredulous astonishment, his spirit rose in a rebellion against arranged facts that was as un-English as it was ungentlemanly. He went back to Solomonson with a mood of thoughtful depression giving place to a growing passion of indignation. He presented it to himself in a generalized and altruistic form. "What the deuce is the good of all this talk of Eugenics," he asked himself aloud, "if they are going to hand over that shining girl to that beastly little area sneak?"

He called Mr. Magnet a "beastly little area sneak!"

Nothing could show more clearly just how much he had contrived to fall in love with Marjorie during his brief sojourn in Buryhamstreet and the acuteness of his disappointment, and nothing could be more eloquent of his forcible and undisciplined temperament. And out of ten thousand possible abusive epithets with which his mind was no doubt stored, this one, I think, had come into his head because of the alert watchfulness with which Mr. Magnet followed a conversation, as he waited his chance for some neat but brilliant flash of comment....

Trafford, like Marjorie, was another of those undisciplined young people our age has produced in such significant quantity. He was just six-and-twenty, but the facts that he was big of build, had as an only child associated much with grown-up people, and was already a conspicuous success in the world of micro-chemical research, had given him the self-reliance and assurance of a much older man. He had still to come his croppers and learn most of the important lessons in life, and, so far, he wasn't aware of it. He was naturally clean-minded, very busy and interested in his work, and on remarkably friendly and confidential terms with his mother who kept house for him, and though he had had several small love disturbances, this was the first occasion that anything of the kind had ploughed deep into his feelings and desires.

Trafford's father had died early in life. He had been a brilliant pathologist, one of that splendid group of scientific investigators in the middle Victorian period which shines ever more brightly as our criticism dims their associated splendours, and he had died before he was thirty through a momentary slip of the scalpel. His wife—she had been his wife for five years—found his child and his memory and the quality of the life he had made about her too satisfying for the risks of a second marriage, and she had brought up her son with a passionate belief in the high mission of research and the supreme duty of seeking out and expressing truth finely. And here he was, calling Mr. Magnet a "beastly little area sneak."

The situation perplexed him. Marjorie perplexed him. It was, had he known it, the beginning for him of a lifetime of problems and perplexities. He was absolutely certain she didn't love Magnet. Why, then, had she agreed to marry him? Such pressures and temptations as he could see about her seemed light to him in comparison with such an undertaking.

Were they greater than he supposed?

His method of coming to the issue of that problem was entirely original. He presented himself next afternoon with the air of an invited guest, drove Mr. Pope who was suffering from liver, to expostulatory sulking in the study, and expressed a passionate craving for golf-croquet, in spite of Mrs. Pope's extreme solicitude for his still bandaged ankle. He was partnered with Daffy, and for a long time he sought speech with Marjorie in vain. At last he was isolated in a corner of the lawn, and with the thinnest pretence of inadvertence, in spite of Daffy's despairing cry of "She plays next!" he laid up within two yards of her. He walked across to her as she addressed herself to her ball, and speaking in an incredulous tone and with the air of a comment on the game, he said: "I say, are you engaged to that chap Magnet?"

Marjorie was amazed, but remarkably not offended. Something in his tone set her trembling. She forgot to play, and stood with her mallet hanging in her hand.

"Punish him!" came the voice of Magnet from afar.

"Yes," she said faintly.

His remark came low and clear. It had a note of angry protest. "Why?"

Marjorie, by the way of answer, hit her ball so that it jumped and missed his, ricochetted across the lawn and out of the ground on the further side.

"I'm sorry if I've annoyed you," said Trafford, as Marjorie went after her ball, and Daffy thanked heaven aloud for the respite.

They came together no more for a time, and Trafford, observant with every sense, found no clue to the riddle of her grave, intent bearing. She played very badly, and with unusual care and deliberation. He felt he had made a mess of things altogether, and suddenly found his leg was too painful to go on. "Partner," he asked, "will you play out my ball for me? I can't go on. I shall have to go."

Marjorie surveyed him, while Daffy and Magnet expressed solicitude. He turned to go, mallet in hand, and found Marjorie following him.

"Is that the heavier mallet?" she asked, and stood before him looking into his eyes and weighing a mallet in either hand.

"Mr. Trafford, you're one of the worst examiners I've ever met," she said.

He looked puzzled.

"I don't know why," said Marjorie, "I wonder as much as you. But I am"; and seeing the light dawning in his eyes, she turned about, and went back to the debacle of her game.

§ 10

After that Mr. Trafford had one clear desire in his being which ruled all his other desires. He wanted a long, frank, unembarrassed and uninterrupted conversation with Marjorie. He had a very strong impression that Marjorie wanted exactly the same thing. For a week he besieged the situation in vain. After the fourth day Solomonson was only kept in Buryhamstreet by sheer will-power, exerted with a brutality that threatened to end that friendship abruptly. He went home on the sixth day in his largest car, but Trafford stayed on beyond the limits of decency to perform some incomprehensible service that he spoke of as "clearing up."

"I want," he said, "to clear up."

"But what is there to clear up, my dear boy?"

"Solomonson, you're a pampered plutocrat," said Trafford, as though everything was explained.

"I don't see any sense in it at all," said Solomonson, and regarded his friend aslant with thick, black eyebrows raised.

"I'm going to stay," said Trafford.

And Solomonson said one of those unhappy and entirely disregarded things that ought never to be said.

"There's some girl in this," said Solomonson.

"Your bedroom's always waiting for you at Riplings," he said, when at last he was going off....

Trafford's conviction that Marjorie also wanted, with an almost equal eagerness, the same opportunity for speech and explanations that he desired, sustained him in a series of unjustifiable intrusions upon the seclusion of the Popes. But although the manner of Mr. and Mrs. Pope did change considerably for the better after his next visit, it was extraordinary how impossible it seemed for him and Marjorie to achieve their common end of an encounter.

Always something intervened.

In the first place, Mrs. Pope's disposition to optimism had got the better of her earlier discretions, and a casual glance at Daphne's face when their visitor reappeared started quite a new thread of interpretations in her mind. She had taken the opportunity of hinting at this when Mr. Pope asked over his shirt-stud that night, "What the devil that—that chauffeur chap meant by always calling in the afternoon."

"Now that Will Magnet monopolizes Marjorie," she said, after a little pause and a rustle or so, "I don't see why Daffy shouldn't have a little company of her own age."

Mr. Pope turned round and stared at her. "I didn't think of that," he said. "But, anyhow, I don't like the fellow."

"He seems to be rather clever," said Mrs. Pope, "though he certainly talks too much. And after all it was Sir Rupert's aeroplane. He was only driving it to oblige."

"He'll think twice before he drives another," said Mr. Pope, wrenching off his collar....

Once Mrs. Pope had turned her imagination in this more and more agreeable direction, she was rather disposed, I am afraid, to let it bolt with her. And it was a deflection that certainly fell in very harmoniously with certain secret speculations of Daphne's. Trafford, too, being quite unused to any sort of social furtiveness, did perhaps, in order to divert attention from his preoccupation with Marjorie, attend more markedly to Daphne than he would otherwise have done. And so presently he found Daphne almost continuously on his hands. So far as she was concerned, he might have told her the entire history of his life, and every secret he had in the world, without let or hindrance. Mrs. Pope, too, showed a growing appreciation of his company, became sympathetic and confidential in a way that invited confidence, and threw a lot of light on her family history and Daffy's character. She had found Daffy a wonderful study, she said. Mr. Pope, too, seemed partly reconciled to him. The idea that, after all, both motor cars and monoplane were Sir Rupert's, and not Trafford's, had produced a reaction in the latter gentleman's favour. Moreover, it had occurred to him that Trafford's accident had perhaps disposed him towards a more thoughtful view of mechanical traction, and that this tendency would be greatly helped by a little genial chaff. So that he ceased to go indoors when Trafford was there, and hung about, meditating and delivering sly digs at this new victim of his ripe, old-fashioned humour.

Nor did it help Trafford in his quest for Marjorie and a free, outspoken delivery that the pseudo-twins considered him a person of very considerable charm, and that

Theodore, though indisposed to "suck up" to him publicly—I write here in Theodorese—did so desire intimate and solitary communion with him, more particularly in view of the chances of an adventitious aeroplane ride that seemed to hang about him—as to stalk him persistently—hovering on the verge of groups, playing a waiting game with a tennis ball and an old racquet, strolling artlessly towards the gate of the avenue when the time seemed ripening for his appearance or departure.

On the other hand, Marjorie was greatly entangled by Magnet.

Magnet was naturally an attentive lover; he was full of small encumbering services, and it made him none the less assiduous to perceive that Marjorie seemed to find no sort of pleasure in all the little things he did. He seemed to think that if picking the very best rose he could find for her did not cause a very perceptible brightening in her, then it was all the more necessary quietly to force her racquet from her hand and carry it for her, or help her ineffectually to cross a foot-wide ditch, or offer to read her in a rich, abundant, well modulated voice, some choice passage from "The Forest Lovers" of Mr. Maurice Hewlett. And behind these devotions there was a streak of jealousy. He knew as if by instinct that it was not wise to leave these two handsome young people together; he had a queer little disagreeable sensation whenever they spoke to one another or looked at one another. Whenever Trafford and Marjorie found themselves in a group, there was Magnet in the midst of them. He knew the value of his Marjorie, and did not mean to lose her....

Being jointly baffled in this way was oddly stimulating to Marjorie's and Trafford's mutual predisposition. If you really want to throw people together, the thing to do—thank God for Ireland!—is to keep them apart. By the fourth day of this emotional incubation, Marjorie was thinking of Trafford to the exclusion of all her reading; and Trafford was lying awake at nights—oh, for half an hour and more—thinking of bold, decisive ways of getting at Marjorie, and bold, decisive things to say to her when he did.

(But why she should be engaged to Magnet continued, nevertheless, to puzzle him extremely. It was a puzzle to which no complete solution was ever to be forthcoming....)

At last that opportunity came. Marjorie had come with her mother into the village, and while Mrs. Pope made some purchases at the general shop she walked on to speak to Mrs. Blythe the washerwoman. Trafford suddenly emerged from the Red Lion with a soda syphon under each arm. She came forward smiling.

"I say," he said forthwith, "I want to talk with you—badly."

"And I," she said unhesitatingly, "with you."

"How can we?"

"There's always people about. It's absurd."

"We'll have to meet."

"Yes."

"I have to go away to-morrow. I ought to have gone two days ago. Where can we meet?"

She had it all prepared.

"Listen," she said. "There is a path runs from our shrubbery through a little wood to a stile on the main road." He nodded. "Either I will be there at three or about half-past five or—there's one more chance. While father and Mr. Magnet are smoking at nine.... I might get away."

"Couldn't I write?"

"No. Impossible."

"I've no end of things to say...."

Mrs. Pope appeared outside her shop, and Trafford gesticulated a greeting with the syphons. "All right," he said to Marjorie. "I'm shopping," he cried as Mrs. Pope approached.

§ 12

All through the day Marjorie desired to go to Trafford and could not do so. It was some minutes past nine when at last with a swift rustle of skirts that sounded louder than all the world to her, she crossed the dimly lit hall between dining-room and drawing-room and came into the dreamland of moonlight upon the lawn. She had told her mother she was going upstairs; at any moment she might be missed, but she would have fled now to Trafford if an army pursued her. Her heart seemed beating in her throat, and every fibre of her being was aquiver. She flitted past the dining-room window like a ghost, she did not dare to glance aside at the smokers within, and round the lawn to the shrubbery, and so under a blackness of trees to the gate where he stood waiting. And there he was, dim and mysterious and wonderful, holding the gate open for her, and she was breathless, and speechless, and near sobbing. She stood before him for a moment, her face moonlit and laced with the shadows of little twigs, and then his arms came out to her.

"My darling," he said, "Oh, my darling!"

They had no doubt of one another or of anything in the world. They clung together; their lips came together fresh and untainted as those first lovers' in the garden.

"I will die for you," he said, "I will give all the world for you...."

They had thought all through the day of a hundred statements and explanations they would make when this moment came, and never a word of it all was uttered. All their anticipations of a highly strung eventful conversation vanished, phrases of the most striking sort went like phantom leaves before a gale. He held her and she clung to him between laughing and sobbing, and both were swiftly and conclusively assured their lives must never separate again.

§ 13

Marjorie never knew whether it was a moment or an age before her father came upon them. He had decided to take a turn in the garden when Magnet could no longer restrain himself from joining the ladies, and he chanced to be stick in hand because that was his habit after twilight. So it was he found them. She heard his voice falling through love and moonlight like something that comes out of an immense distance.

"Good God!" he cried, "what next!"

But he still hadn't realized the worst.

"Daffy," he said, "what in the name of goodness——?"

Marjorie put her hands before her face too late.

"Good Lord!" he cried with a rising inflection,

"it's Madge!"

Trafford found the situation difficult. "I should explain——"

But Mr. Pope was giving himself up to a towering rage. "You damned scoundrel!" he said. "What the devil are you doing?" He seized Marjorie by the arm and drew her towards him. "My poor misguided girl!" he said, and suddenly she was tensely alive, a little cry of horror in her throat, for her father, at a loss for words and full of heroic rage, had suddenly swung his stick with passionate force, and struck at Trafford's face. She heard the thud, saw Trafford wince and stiffen. For a perfectly horrible moment it seemed to her these men, their faces queerly distorted by the shadows of the branches in the slanting moonlight, might fight. Then she heard Trafford's voice, sounding cool and hard, and she knew that he would do nothing of the kind. In that instant if there had remained anything to win in Marjorie it was altogether won. "I asked your daughter to meet me here," he said.

"Be off with you, sir!" cried Mr. Pope. "Don't tempt me further, sir," and swung his stick again. But now the force had gone out of him. Trafford stood with a hand out ready for him, and watched his face.

"I asked your daughter to meet me here, and she came. I am prepared to give you any explanation——"

"If you come near this place again——"

For some moments Marjorie's heart had been held still, now it was beating violently. She felt this scene must end. "Mr. Trafford," she said, "will you go. Go now. Nothing shall keep us apart!"

Mr. Pope turned on her. "Silence, girl!" he said.

"I shall come to you to-morrow," said Trafford.

"Yes," said Marjorie, "to-morrow."

"Marjorie!" said Mr. Pope, "will you go indoors."

"I have done nothing——"

"Be off, sir."

"I have done nothing——"

"Will you be off, sir? And you, Marjorie—will you go indoors?"

He came round upon her, and after one still moment of regard for Trafford—and she looked very beautiful in the moonlight with her hair a little disordered and her face alight—she turned to precede her father through the shrubbery.

Mr. Pope hesitated whether he should remain with Trafford.

A perfectly motionless man is very disconcerting.

"Be off, sir," he said over his shoulder, lowered through a threatening second, and followed her.

But Trafford remained stiffly with a tingling temple down which a little thread of blood was running, until their retreating footsteps had died down into that confused stirring of little sounds which makes the stillness of an English wood at night.

Then he roused himself with a profound sigh, and put a hand to his cut and bruised cheek.

"Well!" he said.

CHAPTER THE FOURTH

Crisis

§ 1

Crisis prevailed in Buryhamstreet that night. On half a dozen sleepless pillows souls communed with the darkness, and two at least of those pillows were wet with tears.

Not one of those wakeful heads was perfectly clear about the origins and bearings of the trouble; not even Mr. Pope felt absolutely sure of himself. It had come as things come to people nowadays, because they will not think things out, much less talk things out, and are therefore in a hopeless tangle of values that tightens sooner or later to a knot....

What an uncharted perplexity, for example, was the mind of that excellent woman Mrs. Pope!

Poor lady! she hadn't a stable thing in her head. It is remarkable that some queer streak in her composition sympathized with Marjorie's passion for Trafford. But she thought it such a pity! She fought that sympathy down as if it were a wicked thing. And she fought too against other ideas that rose out of the deeps and did not so much come into her mind as cluster at the threshold, the idea that Marjorie was in effect grown up, a dozen queer criticisms of Magnet, and a dozen subtle doubts whether after all Marjorie was going to be happy with him as she assured herself the girl would be. (So far as any one knew Trafford might be an excellent match!) And behind these would-be invaders of her guarded mind prowled even worse ones, doubts, horrible disloyal doubts, about the wisdom and kindness of Mr. Pope.

Quite early in life Mrs. Pope had realized that it is necessary to be very careful with one's thoughts. They lead to trouble. She had clipped the wings of her own mind therefore so successfully that all her conclusions had become evasions, all her decisions compromises. Her profoundest working conviction was a belief that nothing in the world was of value but "tact," and that the art of living was to "tide things over." But here it seemed almost beyond her strength to achieve any sort of tiding over....

(Why couldn't Mr. Pope lie quiet?)

Whatever she said or did had to be fitted to the exigencies of Mr. Pope.

Availing himself of the privileges of matrimony, her husband so soon as Mr. Magnet had gone and they were upstairs together, had explained the situation with vivid simplicity, and had gone on at considerable length and with great vivacity to enlarge upon his daughter's behaviour. He ascribed this moral disaster,—he presented it as a moral disaster of absolutely calamitous dimensions—entirely to Mrs. Pope's faults and negligences. Warming with his theme he had employed a number of homely expressions rarely heard by decent women except in these sacred intimacies, to express the deep indignation of a strong man moved to unbridled speech by the wickedness of those near and dear to him. Still warming, he raised his voice and at last shouted out his more forcible meanings, until she feared the servants and children might hear, waved a clenched fist at imaginary Traffords and scoundrels generally, and giving way completely to his outraged virtue, smote and kicked blameless articles of furniture in a manner deeply impressive to the feminine intelligence.

Finally he sat down in the little arm-chair between her and the cupboard where she was accustomed to hang up her clothes, stuck out his legs very stiffly across the room, and despaired of his family in an obtrusive and impregnable silence for an enormous time.

All of which awakened a deep sense of guilt and unworthiness in Mrs. Pope's mind, and prevented her going to bed, but did not help her in the slightest degree to grasp the difficulties of the situation....

She would have lain awake anyhow, but she was greatly helped in this by Mr. Pope's restlessness. He was now turning over from left to right or from right to left at intervals of from four to seven minutes, and such remarks as "Damned scoundrel! Get out of this!" or "My daughter and degrade yourself in this way!" or "Never let me see your face again!" "Plight your troth to one man, and fling yourself shamelessly—I repeat it, Marjorie, shamelessly—into the arms of another!" kept Mrs. Pope closely in touch with the general trend of his thoughts.

She tried to get together her plans and perceptions rather as though she swept up dead leaves on a gusty day. She knew that the management of the whole situation rested finally on her, and that whatever she did or did not do, or whatever arose to thwart her arrangements, its entire tale of responsibility would ultimately fall upon her shoulders. She wondered what was to be done with Marjorie, with Mr. Magnet? Need he know? Could that situation be saved? Everything at present was raw in her mind. Except for her husband's informal communications she did not even know what had appeared, what Daffy had seen, what Magnet thought of Marjorie's failure to bid him good-night. For example, had Mr. Magnet noticed Mr. Pope's profound disturbance? She had to be ready to put a face on things before morning, and it seemed impossible she could do so. In times of crisis, as every woman knows, it is always necessary to misrepresent everything to everybody, but how she was to dovetail her misrepresentations, get the best effect from them, extract a working system of rights and wrongs from them, she could not imagine....

(Oh! she did so wish Mr. Pope would lie quiet.)

But he had no doubts of what became him. He had to maintain a splendid and irrational rage—at any cost—to anybody.

§ 2

A few yards away, a wakeful Marjorie confronted a joyless universe. She had a baffling realization that her life was in a hopeless mess, that she really had behaved disgracefully, and that she couldn't for a moment understand how it had happened. She had intended to make quite sure of Trafford—and then put things straight.

Only her father had spoilt everything.

She regarded her father that night with a want of natural affection terrible to record. Why had he come just when he had, just as he had? Why had he been so violent, so impossible?

Of course, she had no business to be there....

She examined her character with a new unprecedented detachment. Wasn't she, after all, rather a mean human being? It had never occurred to her before to ask such a question. Now she asked it with only too clear a sense of the answer. She tried to trace how these multiplying threads of meanness had first come into the fabric of a life she had supposed herself to be weaving in extremely bright, honourable, and adventurous colours. She ought, of course, never to have accepted Magnet....

She faced the disagreeable word; was she a liar?

At any rate, she told lies.

And she'd behaved with extraordinary meanness to Daphne. She realized that now. She had known, as precisely as if she had been told, how Daphne felt about Trafford, and she'd never given her an inkling of her own relations. She hadn't for a moment thought of Daphne. No wonder Daffy was sombre and bitter. Whatever she knew, she knew enough. She had heard Trafford's name in urgent whispers on the landing. "I suppose you couldn't leave him alone," Daffy had said, after a long hostile silence. That was all. Just a sentence without prelude or answer flung across the bedroom, revealing a perfect understanding—deeps of angry disillusionment. Marjorie had stared and gasped, and made no answer.

Would she ever see him again? After this horror of rowdy intervention? She didn't deserve to; she didn't deserve anything.... Oh, the tangle of it all! The tangle of it all! And those bills at Oxbridge! She was just dragging Trafford down into her own miserable morass of a life.

Her thoughts would take a new turn. "I love him," she whispered soundlessly. "I would die for him. I would like to lie under his feet—and him not know it."

Her mind hung on that for a long time. "Not know it until afterwards," she corrected.

She liked to be exact, even in despair....

And then in her memory he was struck again, and stood stiff and still. She wanted to kneel to him, imagined herself kneeling....

And so on, quite inconclusively, round and round through the interminable night hours.

§ 3

The young man in the village was, if possible, more perplexed, round-eyed and generally inconclusive than anyone else in this series of nocturnal disturbances. He spent long intervals sitting on his window-sill regarding a world that was scented with nightstock, and seemed to be woven of moonshine and gossamer. Being an inexpert and infrequent soliloquist, his only audible comment on his difficulties was the repetition in varying intonations of his fervent, unalterable conviction that he was damned. But behind this simple verbal mask was a great fury of mental activity.

He had something of Marjorie's amazement at the position of affairs.

He had never properly realized that it was possible for any one to regard Marjorie as a daughter, to order her about and resent the research for her society as criminal. It was a new light in his world. Some day he was to learn the meaning of fatherhood, but in these night watches he regarded it as a hideous survival of mediæval darknesses.

"Of course," he said, entirely ignoring the actual quality of their conversation, "she had to explain about the Magnet affair. Can't one—converse?"

He reflected through great intervals.

"I will see her! Why on earth shouldn't I see her?"

"I suppose they can't lock her up!"

For a time he contemplated a writ of Habeas Corpus. He saw reason to regret the gaps in his legal knowledge.

"Can any one get a writ of Habeas Corpus for any one—it doesn't matter whom"—more especially if you are a young man of six-and-twenty, anxious to exchange a few richly charged words with a girl of twenty who is engaged to someone else?

The night had no answer.

It was nearly dawn when he came to the entirely inadvisable conclusion—I use his own word's—to go and have it out with the old ruffian. He would sit down and ask him what he meant by it all—and reason with him. If he started flourishing that stick again, it would have to be taken away.

And having composed a peroration upon the institution of the family of a character which he fondly supposed to be extraordinarily tolerant, reasonable and convincing, but which was indeed calculated to madden Mr. Pope to frenzy, Mr. Trafford went very peacefully to sleep.

§ 4

Came dawn, with a noise of birds and afterwards a little sleep, and then day, and heavy eyes opened again, and the sound of frying and the smell of coffee recalled our actors to the stage. Mrs. Pope was past her worst despair; always the morning brings courage and a clearer grasp of things, and she could face the world with plans shaped subconsciously during those last healing moments of slumber.

Breakfast was difficult, but not impossible. Mr. Pope loomed like a thundercloud, but Marjorie pleaded a headache very wisely, and was taken a sympathetic cup of tea. The pseudo-twins scented trouble, but Theodore was heedless and over-full of an entertaining noise made by a moorhen as it dived in the ornamental water that morning. You could make it practically sotto voce, and it amused Syd. He seemed to think the Times opaque to such small sounds, and learnt better only to be dismissed underfed and ignominiously from the table to meditate upon the imperfections of his soul in the schoolroom. There for a time he was silent, and then presently became audible again, playing with a ball and, presumably, Marjorie's tennis racquet.

Directly she could disentangle herself from breakfast Mrs. Pope, with all her plans acute, went up to the girls' room. She found her daughter dressing in a leisurely and meditative manner. She shut the door almost confidentially. "Marjorie," she said, "I want you to tell me all about this."

"I thought I heard father telling you," said Marjorie.

"He was too indignant," said Mrs. Pope, "to explain clearly. You see, Marjorie"—she paused before her effort—"he knows things—about this Professor Trafford."

"What things?" asked Marjorie, turning sharply.

"I don't know, my dear—and I can't imagine."

She looked out of the window, aware of Marjorie's entirely distrustful scrutiny.

"I don't believe it," said Marjorie.

"Don't believe what, dear?"

"Whatever he says."

"I wish I didn't," said Mrs. Pope, and turned. "Oh, Madge," she cried, "you cannot imagine how all this distresses me! I cannot—I cannot conceive how you came to be in such a position! Surely honour——! Think of Mr. Magnet, how good and patient he has been! You don't know that man. You don't know all he is, and all that it means to a girl. He is good and honourable and—pure. He is kindness itself. It seemed to me that you were to be so happy—rich, honoured."

She was overcome by a rush of emotion; she turned to the bed and sat down.

"There!" she said desolately. "It's all ruined, shattered, gone."

Marjorie tried not to feel that her mother was right.

"If father hadn't interfered," she said weakly.

"Oh, don't, my dear, speak so coldly of your father! You don't know what he has to put up with. You don't know his troubles and anxieties—all this wretched business." She paused, and her face became portentous. "Marjorie, do you know if these railways go on as they are going he may have to eat into his capital this year. Just think of that, and the worry he has! And this last shame and anxiety!"

Her voice broke again. Marjorie listened with an expression that was almost sullen.

"But what is it," she asked, "that father knows about Mr. Trafford?"

"I don't know, dear. I don't know. But it's something that matters—that makes it all different."

"Well, may I speak to Mr. Trafford before he leaves Buryhamstreet?"

"My dear! Never see him, dear—never think of him again! Your father would not dream——Some day, Marjorie, you will rejoice—you will want to thank your father on your bended knees that he saved you from the clutches of this man...."

"I won't believe anything about Mr. Trafford," she said slowly, "until I know——"

She left the sentence incomplete.

She made her declaration abruptly. "I love Mr. Trafford," she said, with a catch in her voice, "and I don't love Mr. Magnet."

Mrs. Pope received this like one who is suddenly stabbed. She sat still as if overwhelmed, one hand pressed to her side and her eyes closed. Then she said, as if she gasped involuntarily—

"It's too dreadful! Marjorie," she said, "I want to ask you to do something. After all, a mother has some claim. Will you wait just a little. Will you promise me to do nothing—nothing, I mean, to commit you—until your father has been able to make inquiries. Don't see him for a little while. Very soon you'll be one-and-twenty, and then perhaps things may be different. If he cares for you, and you for him, a little separation won't matter.... Until your father has inquired...."

"Mother," said Marjorie, "I can't——"

Mrs. Pope drew in the air sharply between her teeth, as if in agony.

"But, mother——Mother, I must let Mr. Trafford know that I'm not to see him. I can't suddenly cease.... If I could see him once——"

"Don't!" said Mrs. Pope, in a hollow voice.

Marjorie began weeping. "He'd not understand," she said. "If I might just speak to him!"

"Not alone, Marjorie."

Marjorie stood still. "Well—before you."

Mrs. Pope conceded the point. "And then, Marjorie——" she said.

"I'd keep my word, mother," said Marjorie, and began to sob in a manner she felt to be absurdly childish—"until—until I am one-and-twenty. I'd promise that."

Mrs. Pope did a brief calculation. "Marjorie," she said, "it's only your happiness I think of."

"I know," said Marjorie, and added in a low voice, "and father."

"My dear, you don't understand your father.... I believe—I do firmly believe—if anything happened to any of you girls—anything bad—he would kill himself.... And I know he means that you aren't to go about so much as you used to do, unless we have the most definite promises. Of course, your father's ideas aren't always my ideas, Marjorie; but it's your duty—You know how hasty he is and—quick. Just as you know how good and generous and kind he is"—she caught Marjorie's eye, and added a little lamely—"at bottom." ... She thought. "I think I could get him to let you say just one word with Mr. Trafford. It would be very difficult, but——"

She paused for a few seconds, and seemed to be thinking deeply.

"Marjorie," she said, "Mr. Magnet must never know anything of this."

"But, mother——!"

"Nothing!"

"I can't go on with my engagement!"

Mrs. Pope shook her head inscrutably.

"But how can I, mother?"

"You need not tell him why, Marjorie."

"But——"

"Just think how it would humiliate and distress him! You can't, Marjorie. You must find some excuse—oh, any excuse! But not the truth—not the truth, Marjorie. It would be too dreadful."

Marjorie thought. "Look here, mother, I may see Mr. Trafford again? I may really speak to him?"

"Haven't I promised?"

"Then, I'll do as you say," said Marjorie.

§ 5

Mrs. Pope found her husband seated at the desk in the ultra-Protestant study, meditating gloomily.

"I've been talking to her," she said, "She's in a state of terrible distress."

"She ought to be," said Mr. Pope.

"Philip, you don't understand Marjorie."

"I don't."

"You think she was kissing that man."

"Well, she was."

"You can think that of her!"

Mr. Pope turned his chair to her. "But I saw!"

Mrs. Pope shook her head. "She wasn't; she was struggling to get away from him. She told me so herself. I've been into it with her. You don't understand, Philip. A man like that has a sort of fascination for a girl. He dazzles her. It's the way with girls. But you're quite mistaken.... Quite. It's a sort of hypnotism. She'll grow out of it. Of course, she loves Mr. Magnet. She does indeed. I've not a doubt of it. But——"

"You're sure she wasn't kissing him?"

"Positive."

"Then why didn't you say so?"

"A girl's so complex. You didn't give her a chance. She's fearfully ashamed of herself—fearfully! but it's just because she is ashamed that she won't admit it."

"I'll make her admit it."

"You ought to have had all boys," said Mrs. Pope. "Oh! she'll admit it some day—readily enough. But I believe a girl of her spirit would rather die than begin explaining. You can't expect it of her. Really you can't."

He grunted and shook his head slowly from side to side.

She sat down in the arm-chair beside the desk.

"I want to know just exactly what we are to do about the girl, Philip. I can't bear to think of her—up there."

"How?" he asked. "Up there?"

"Yes," she answered with that skilful inconsecutiveness of hers, and let a brief silence touch his imagination. "Do you think that man means to come here again?" she asked.

"Chuck him out if he does," said Mr. Pope, grimly.

She pressed her lips together firmly. She seemed to be weighing things painfully. "I wouldn't," she said at last.

"What do you mean?" asked Mr. Pope.

"I do not want you to make an open quarrel with Mr. Trafford."

"Not quarrel!"

"Not an open one," said Mrs. Pope. "Of course I know how nice it would be if you could use a horsewhip, dear. There's such a lot of things—if we only just slash. But—it won't help. Get him to go away. She's consented never to see him again—practically. She's ready to tell him so herself. Part them against their will—oh! and the thing may go on for no end of time. But treat it as it ought to be treated—She'll be very tragic for a week or so, and then she'll forget him like a dream. He is a dream—a girl's dream.... If only we leave it alone, she'll leave it alone."

§ 6

Things were getting straight, Mrs. Pope felt. She had now merely to add a few touches to the tranquillization of Daphne, and the misdirection of the twin's curiosity. These touches accomplished, it seemed that everything was done. After a brief reflection, she dismissed the idea of putting things to Theodore. She ran over the possibilities of the servants eavesdropping, and found them negligible. Yes, everything was done—everything. And yet....

The queer string in her nature between religiosity and superstition began to vibrate. She hesitated. Then she slipped upstairs, fastened the door, fell on her knees beside the bed and put the whole thing as acceptably as possible to Heaven in a silent, simple, but lucidly explanatory prayer....

She came out of her chamber brighter and braver than she had been for eighteen long hours. She could now, she felt, await the developments that threatened with the serenity of one who is prepared at every point. She went almost happily to the kitchen, only about forty-five minutes behind her usual time, to order the day's meals and see with her own eyes that economies prevailed. And it seemed to her, on the whole, consoling, and at any rate a distraction, when the cook informed her that after all she had meant to give notice on the day of aunt Plessington's visit.

§ 7

The unsuspecting Magnet, fatigued but happy—for three hours of solid humorous writing (omitting every unpleasant suggestion and mingling in the most acceptable and saleable proportions smiles and tears) had added its quota to the intellectual heritage of England, made a simple light lunch cooked in homely village-inn fashion, lit a well merited cigar, and turned his steps towards the vicarage. He was preceded at some distance along the avenuesque drive by the back of Mr. Trafford, which he made no attempt to overtake.

Mr. Trafford was admitted and disappeared, and a minute afterwards Magnet reached the door.

Mrs. Pope appeared radiant—about the weather. A rather tiresome man had just called upon Mr. Pope about business matters, she said, and he might be detained five or ten minutes. Marjorie and Daffy were upstairs—resting. They had been disturbed by bats in the night.

"Isn't it charmingly rural?" said Mrs. Pope. "Bats!"

She talked about bats and the fear she had of their getting in her hair, and as she talked she led the way brightly but firmly as far as possible out of earshot of the windows of the ultra Protestant study in which Mr. Pope was now (she did so hope temperately) interviewing Mr. Trafford.

§ 8

Directly Mr. Trafford had reached the front door it had opened for him, and closed behind him at once. He had found himself with Mrs. Pope. "You wish to see my husband?" she had said, and had led him to the study forthwith. She had returned at once to intercept Mr. Magnet....

Trafford found Mr. Pope seated sternly at the centre of the writing desk, regarding him with a threatening brow.

"Well, sir," said Mr. Pope breaking the silence, "you have come to offer some explanation——"

While awaiting this encounter Mr. Pope had not been insensitive to the tactical and scenic possibilities of the occasion. In fact, he had spent the latter half of the morning in intermittent preparations, arranging desks, books, hassocks in advantageous positions, and not even neglecting such small details as the stamp tray, the articles of interest from Jerusalem, and the rock-crystal cenotaph, which he had exhibited in such a manner as was most calculated to damp, chill and subjugate an antagonist in the exposed area towards the window. He had also arranged the chairs in a highly favourable pattern.

Mr. Trafford was greatly taken aback by Mr. Pope's juridical manner and by this form of address, and he was further put out by Mr. Pope saying with a regal gesture to the best illuminated and most isolated chair: "Be seated, sir."

Mr. Trafford's exordium vanished from his mind, he was at a loss for words until spurred to speech by Mr. Pope's almost truculent: "Well?"

"I am in love sir, with your daughter."

"I am not aware of it," said Mr. Pope, and lifted and dropped the paper-weight. "My daughter, sir, is engaged to marry Mr. Magnet. If you had approached me in a proper fashion before presuming to attempt—to attempt——" His voice thickened with indignation,—"Liberties with her, you would have been duly informed of her position—and everyone would have been saved"—he lifted the paper-weight. "Everything that has happened." (Bump.)

Mr. Trafford had to adjust himself to the unexpected elements in this encounter. "Oh!" he said.

"Yes," said Mr. Pope, and there was a distinct interval.

"Is your daughter in love with Mr. Magnet?" asked Mr. Trafford in an almost colloquial tone.

Mr. Pope smiled gravely. "I presume so, sir."

"She never gave me that impression, anyhow," said the young man.

"It was neither her duty to give nor yours to receive that impression," said Mr. Pope.

Again Mr. Trafford was at a loss.

"Have you come here, sir, merely to bandy words?" asked Mr. Pope, drumming with ten fingers on the table.

Mr. Trafford thrust his hands into his pockets and assumed a fictitious pose of ease. He had never found any one in his life before quite so provocative of colloquialism as Mr. Pope.

"Look here, sir, this is all very well," he began, "but why can't I fall in love with your daughter? I'm a Doctor of Science and all that sort of thing. I've a perfectly decent outlook. My father was rather a swell in his science. I'm an entirely decent and respectable person."

"I beg to differ," said Mr. Pope.

"But I am."

"Again," said Mr. Pope, with great patience, and a slight forward bowing of the head, "I beg to differ."

"Well—differ. But all the same——"

He paused and began again, and for a time they argued to no purpose. They generalized about the position of an engaged girl and the rights and privileges of a father. Then Mr. Pope, "to cut all this short," told him frankly he wasn't wanted, his daughter did not want him, nobody wanted him; he was an invader, he had to be got rid of—"if possible by peaceful means." Trafford disputed these propositions, and asked to see Marjorie. Mr. Pope had been leading up to this, and at once closed with that request.

"She is as anxious as any one to end this intolerable siege," he said. He went to the door and called for Marjorie, who appeared with conspicuous promptitude. She was in a dress of green linen that made her seem very cool as well as very dignified to Trafford; she was tense with restrained excitement, and either—for these things shade into each other—entirely without a disposition to act her part or acting with consummate ability. Trafford rose at the sight of her, and remained standing. Mr. Pope closed the door and walked back to the desk. "Mr. Trafford has to be told," he said, "that you don't want him in Buryhamstreet." He arrested Marjorie's forward movement towards Trafford by a gesture of the hand, seated himself, and resumed his drumming on the table. "Well?" he said.

"I don't think you ought to stay in Buryhamstreet, Mr. Trafford," said Marjorie.

"You don't want me to?"

"It will only cause trouble—and scenes."

"You want me to go?"

"Away from here."

"You really mean that?"

Marjorie did not answer for a little time; she seemed to be weighing the exact force of all she was going to say.

"Mr. Trafford," she answered, "everything I've ever said to you—everything—I've meant, more than I've ever meant anything. Everything!"

A little flush of colour came into Trafford's cheeks. He regarded Marjorie with a brightening eye.

"Oh well," he said, "I don't understand. But I'm entirely in your hands, of course."

Marjorie's pose and expression altered. For an instant she was a miracle of instinctive expression, she shone at him, she conveyed herself to him, she assured him. Her eyes met his, she stood warmly flushed and quite unconquered—visibly, magnificently his. She poured into him just that riotous pride and admiration that gives a man altogether to a woman.... Then it seemed as if a light passed, and she was just an everyday Marjorie standing there.

"I'll do anything you want me to," said Trafford.

"Then I want you to go."

"Ah!" said Mr. Pope.

"Yes," said Trafford, with his eyes on her self-possession.

"I've promised not to write or send to you, or—think more than I can help of you, until I'm twenty-one—nearly two months from now."

"And then?"

"I don't know. How can I?"

"You hear, sir?" from Mr. Pope, in the pause of mutual scrutiny that followed.

"One question," said Mr. Trafford.

"You've surely asked enough, sir," said Mr. Pope.

"Are you still engaged to Magnet?"

"Sir!"

"Please, father;" said Marjorie, with unusual daring and in her mother's voice. "Mr. Trafford, after what I've told you—you must leave that to me."

"She is engaged to Mr. Magnet," said Mr. Pope. "Tell him outright, Marjorie. Make it clear."

"I think I understand," said Trafford, with his eyes on Marjorie.

"I've not seen Mr. Magnet since last night," said Marjorie. "And so—naturally—I'm still engaged to him."

"Precisely!" said Mr. Pope, and turned with a face of harsh interrogation to his importunate caller. Mr. Trafford seemed disposed for further questions. "I don't think we need detain you, Madge," said Mr. Pope, over his shoulder.

The two young people stood facing one another for a moment, and I am afraid that they were both extremely happy and satisfied with each other. It was all right, they were quite sure—all right. Their lips were almost smiling. Then Marjorie made an entirely dignified exit. She closed the door very softly, and Mr. Pope turned to his visitor again with a bleak politeness. "I hope that satisfies you," he said.

"There is nothing more to be said at present, I admit," said Mr. Trafford.

"Nothing," said Mr. Pope.

Both gentlemen bowed. Mr. Pope rose ceremoniously, and Mr. Trafford walked doorward. He had a sense of latent absurdities in these tremendous attitudes. They passed through the hall—processionally. But just at the end some lower strain in Mr. Trafford's nature touched the fine dignity of the occasion with an inappropriate remark.

"Good-bye, sir," said Mr. Pope, holding the housedoor wide.

"Good-bye, sir," said Mr. Trafford, and then added with a note of untimely intimacy in his voice, with an inexcusable levity upon his lips: "You know—there's nobody—no man in the world—I'd sooner have for a father-in-law than you."

Mr. Pope, caught unprepared on the spur of the moment, bowed in a cold and distant manner, and then almost immediately closed the door to save himself from violence....

From first to last neither gentleman had made the slightest allusion to a considerable bruise upon Mr. Trafford's left cheek, and a large abrasion above his ear.

§ 9

That afternoon Marjorie began her difficult task of getting disengaged from Mr. Magnet. It was difficult because she was pledged not to tell him of the one thing that made this line of action not only explicable, but necessary. Magnet, perplexed, and disconcerted, and secretly sustained by her mother's glancing sidelights on the feminine character and the instability of "girlish whims," remained at Buryhamstreet until the family returned to Hartstone Square. The engagement was ended— formally—but in such a manner that Magnet was left a rather pathetic and invincibly assiduous besieger. He lavished little presents upon both sisters, he devised little treats for the entire family, he enriched Theodore beyond the dreams of avarice, and he discussed his love and admiration for Marjorie, and the perplexities and delicacies of the situation not only with Mrs. Pope, but with Daphne. At first he had thought very little of Daphne, but now he was beginning to experience the subtle pleasures of a confidential friendship. She understood, he felt; it was quite wonderful how she understood. He found Daffy much richer in response than Marjorie, and far less disconcerting in reply....

Mr. Pope, for all Marjorie's submission to his wishes, developed a Grand Dudgeon of exceptionally fine proportions when he heard of the breach of the engagement. He ceased to speak to his daughter or admit himself aware of her existence, and the Grand Dudgeon's blighting shadow threw a chill over the life of every one in the house. He made it clear that the Grand Dudgeon would only be lifted by Marjorie's re-engagement to Magnet, and that whatever blight or inconvenience fell on the others was due entirely to Marjorie's wicked obstinacy. Using Mrs. Pope as an intermediary, he also conveyed to Marjorie his decision to be no longer burthened with the charges of her education at Oxbridge, and he made it seem extremely doubtful whether he should remember her approaching twenty-first birthday.

Marjorie received the news of her severance from Oxbridge, Mrs. Pope thought, with a certain hardness.

"I thought he would do that," said Marjorie. "He's always wanted to do that," and said no more.

CHAPTER THE FIFTH

A Telephone Call

§ 1

Trafford went back to Solomonson for a day or so, and then to London, to resume the experimental work of the research he had in hand. But he was so much in love with Marjorie that for some days it was a very dazed mind that fumbled with the apparatus—arranged it and rearranged it, and fell into daydreams that gave the utmost concern to Durgan the bottle-washer.

"He's not going straight at things," said Durgan the bottle-washer to his wife. "He usually goes so straight at things it's a pleasure to watch it. He told me he was going down into Kent to think everything out." Mr. Durgan paused impressively, and spoke with a sigh of perplexity. "He hasn't...."

But later Durgan was able to report that Trafford had pulled himself together. The work was moving.

"I was worried for a bit," said Mr. Durgan. "But I think it's all right again. I believe it's all right again."

§ 2

Trafford was one of those rare scientific men who really ought to be engaged in scientific research.

He could never leave an accepted formula alone. His mind was like some insatiable corrosive, that ate into all the hidden inequalities and plastered weaknesses of accepted theories, and bit its way through every plausibility of appearance. He was extraordinarily fertile in exasperating alternative hypotheses. His invention of destructive test experiments was as happy as the respectful irony with which he brought them into contact with the generalizations they doomed. He was already, at six-and-twenty, hated, abused, obstructed, and respected. He was still outside the Royal Society, of course, and the editors of the scientific periodicals admired his papers greatly, and delayed publication; but it was fairly certain that that pressure of foreign criticism and competition which prevents English scientific men of good family and social position from maintaining any such national standards as we are able to do in art, literature, and politics, would finally carry him in. And since he had a small professorship worth three hundred a year, which gave him the command of a sufficient research laboratory and the services of Mr. Durgan, a private income of nearly three hundred more, a devoted mother to keep house for him, and an invincible faith in Truth, he had every prospect of winning in his particular struggle to inflict more Truth, new lucidities, and fresh powers upon this fractious and unreasonable universe.

In the world of science now, even more than in the world of literature and political thought, the thing that is alive struggles, half-suffocated, amidst a copious production of things born dead. The endowment of research, the organization of scientific progress, the creation of salaried posts, and the assignment of honours, has attracted to this field just that type of man which is least gifted to penetrate and discover, and least able to admit its own defect or the quality of a superior. Such men are producing great, bulky masses of imitative research, futile inquiries, and monstrous entanglements of technicality about their subjects; and it is to their instinctive antagonism to the idea of a "gift" in such things that we owe the preposterous conception of a training for research, the manufacture of mental blinkers that is to say, to avoid what is the very soul of brilliant inquiry—applicable discursiveness. The trained investigator is quite the absurdest figure in the farce of contemporary intellectual life; he is like a bath-chair perpetually starting to cross the Himalayas by virtue of a licence to do so. For such enterprises one must have wings. Organization and genius are antipathetic. The vivid and creative mind, by virtue of its qualities, is a spasmodic and adventurous mind; it resents blinkers, and the mere implication that it can be driven in harness to the unexpected. It demands freedom. It resents regular attendance from ten to four and punctualities in general and all those paralyzing minor tests of conduct that are vitally important to the imagination of the authoritative dull. Consequently, it is being eliminated from its legitimate field, and it is only here and there among the younger men that such a figure as Trafford gives any promise of a renewal of that enthusiasm, that intellectual enterprise, which were distinctive of the great age of scientific advance.

Trafford was the only son of his parents. His father had been a young surgeon, more attracted by knowledge than practice, who had been killed by a scratch of the scalpel in an investigation upon ulcerative processes, at the age of twenty-nine. Trafford at that time was three years old, so that he had not the least memory of his father; but his mother, by a thousand almost unpremeditated touches, had built up a figure for him and a tradition that was shaping his life. She had loved her husband passionately, and when he died her love burnt up like a flame released, and made a god of the good she had known with him.

She was then a very beautiful and active-minded woman of thirty, and she did her best to reconstruct her life; but she could find nothing so living in the world as the clear courage, the essential simplicity, and tender memories of the man she had lost. And she was the more devoted to him that he had had little weaknesses of temper and bearing, and that an outrageous campaign had been waged against him that did not cease with his death. He had, in some medical periodical, published drawings of a dead dog clamped to display a deformity, and these had been seized upon by a group of anti-vivisection fanatics as the representation of a vivisection. A libel action had been pending when he died; but there is no protection of the dead from libel. That monstrous lie met her on pamphlet cover, on hoardings, in sensational appeals; it seemed immortal, and she would have suffered the pains of a dozen suttees if she could have done so, to show the world how the power and tenderness of this alleged tormentor of helpless beasts had gripped one woman's heart. It counted enormously in her decision to remain a widow and concentrate her life upon her son.

She watched his growth with a care and passionate subtlety that even at six-and-twenty he was still far from suspecting. She dreaded his becoming a mother's pet, she sent him away to school and fretted through long terms alone, that he might be made into a man. She interested herself in literary work and social affairs lest she should press upon him unduly. She listened for the crude expression of growing thought in him with an intensity that was almost anguish. She was too intelligent to dream of forming his mind, he browsed on every doctrine to find his own, but she did desire most passionately, she prayed, she prayed in the darkness of sleepless nights, that the views, the breadths, the spacious emotions which had ennobled her husband in her eyes should rise again in him.

There were years of doubt and waiting. He was a good boy and a bad boy, now brilliant, now touching, now disappointing, now gloriously reassuring, and now heart-rending as only the children of our blood can be. He had errors and bad moments, lapses into sheer naughtiness, phases of indolence, attacks of contagious vulgarity. But more and more surely she saw him for his father's son; she traced the same great curiosities, the same keen dauntless questioning; whatever incidents might disturb and perplex her, his intellectual growth went on strong and clear and increasing like some sacred flame that is carried in procession, halting perhaps and swaying a little but keeping on, over the heads of a tumultuous crowd.

He went from his school to the Royal College of Science, thence to successes at Cambridge, and thence to Berlin. He travelled a little in Asia Minor and Persia, had a journey to America, and then came back to her and London, sunburnt, moustached, manly, and a little strange. When he had been a boy she had thought his very soul pellucid; it had clouded opaquely against her scrutiny as he passed into adolescence. Then through the period of visits and departures, travel together, separations, he grew into something detached and admirable, a man curiously reminiscent of his father, unexpectedly different. She ceased to feel what he was feeling in his mind, had to watch him, infer, guess, speculate about him. She desired for him and dreaded for him with an undying tenderness, but she no longer had any assurance that she could interfere to help him. He had his father's trick of falling into thought. Her brown eyes would watch him across the flowers and delicate glass and silver of her dinner table when he dined at home with her. Sometimes he seemed to forget she existed, sometimes he delighted in her, talked to amuse her, petted her; sometimes, and then it was she was happiest, he talked of plays and books with her, discussed general questions, spoke even of that broadly conceived scheme of work which engaged so much of his imagination. She knew that it was distinguished and powerful work. Old friends of her husband spoke of it to her, praised its inspired directness, its beautiful simplicity. Since the days of Wollaston, they said, no one had been so witty an experimenter, no one had got more out of mere scraps of apparatus or contrived more ingenious simplifications.

When he had accepted the minor Professorship which gave him a footing in the world of responsible scientific men, she had taken a house in a quiet street in Chelsea which necessitated a daily walk to his laboratory. It was a little old Georgian house with worn and graceful rooms, a dignified front door and a fine gateway of Sussex ironwork much painted and eaten away. She arranged it with great care; she had kept most of her furniture, and his study had his father's bureau, and the selfsame agate paper-weight that had pressed the unfinished paper he left when he died. She was a woman of persistent friendships, and there came to her, old connections of those early times trailing fresher and younger people in their wake, sons, daughters, nephews, disciples; her son brought home all sorts of interesting men, and it was remarkable to her that amidst the talk and discussion at her table, she discovered aspects of her son and often quite intimate aspects she would never have seen with him alone.

She would not let herself believe that this Indian summer of her life could last for ever. He was no passionless devotee of research, for all his silence and restraints. She had seen him kindle with anger at obstacles and absurdities, and quicken in the presence of beauty. She knew how readily and richly he responded to beauty. Things happened to have run smoothly with him so far, that was all. "Of course," she said, "he must fall in love. It cannot be long before he falls in love."

Once or twice that had seemed to happen, and then it had come to nothing....

She knew that sooner or later this completion of his possibilities must come, that the present steadfastness of purpose was a phase in which forces gathered, that love must sweep into his life as a deep and passionate disturbance. She wondered where it would take him, whether it would leave him enriched or devastated. She saw at times how young he was; she had, as I suppose most older people have about their juniors, the profoundest doubt whether he was wise enough yet to be trusted with a thing so good as himself. He had flashes of high-spirited indiscretion, and at times a wildfire of humour flared in his talk. So far that had done no worse for him than make an enemy or so in scientific circles. But she had no idea of the limits of his excitability. She would watch him and fear for him—she knew the wreckage love can make—and also she desired that he should lose nothing that life and his nature could give him.

§ 3

In the two months of separation that ensued before Marjorie was one-and-twenty, Trafford's mind went through some remarkable phases. At first the excitement of his passion for Marjorie obscured everything else, then with his return to London and his laboratory the immense inertia of habit and slowly developed purposes, the complex yet convergent system of ideas and problems to which so much of his life had been given, began to reassert itself. His love was vivid and intense, a light in his imagination, a fever in his blood; but it was a new thing; it had not crept into the flesh and bones of his being, it was away there in Surrey; the streets of London, his home, the white-walled chamber with its skylight and high windows and charts of constants, in which his apparatus was arranged, had no suggestion of her. She was outside—an adventure—a perplexing incommensurable with all these things.

He had left Buryhamstreet with Marjorie riotously in possession of his mind. He could think of nothing but Marjorie in the train, and how she had shone at him in the study, and how her voice had sounded when she spoke, and how she stood and moved, and the shape and sensation of her hands, and how it had felt to hold her for those brief moments in the wood and press lips and body to his, and how her face had gleamed in the laced shadows of the moonlight, soft and wonderful.

In fact, he thought of Marjorie.

He thought she was splendid, courageous, wise by instinct. He had no doubt of her or that she was to be his—when the weeks of waiting had passed by. She was his, and he was Marjorie's; that had been settled from the beginning of the world. It didn't occur to him that anything had happened to alter his life or any of his arrangements in any way, except that they were altogether altered—as the world is altered without displacement when the sun pours up in the east. He was glorified—and everything was glorified.

He wondered how they would meet again, and dreamt a thousand impossible and stirring dreams, but he dreamt them as dreams.

At first, to Durgan's infinite distress, he thought of her all day, and then, as the old familiar interests grappled him again, he thought of her in the morning and the evening and as he walked between his home and the laboratory and at all sorts of incidental times—and even when the close-locked riddles of his research held the foreground and focus of his thoughts, he still seemed to be thinking of her as a radiant background to ions and molecules and atoms and interwoven systems of eddies and quivering oscillations deep down in the very heart of matter.

And always he thought of her as something of the summer. The rich decays of autumn came, the Chelsea roads were littered with variegated leaves that were presently wet and dirty and slippery, the twilight crept down into the day towards five o'clock and four, but in his memory of her the leaves were green, the evenings were long, the warm quiet of rural Surrey in high August filled the air. So that it was with a kind of amazement he found her in London and in November close at hand. He was called to the college telephone one day from a conversation with a proposed research student. It was a middle-aged woman bachelor anxious for the D.Sc., who wished to occupy the further bench in the laboratory; but she had no mental fire, and his mind was busy with excuses and discouragements.

He had no thought of Marjorie when she answered, and for an instant he did not recognize her voice.

"Yes, I'm Mr. Trafford."...

"Who is it?" he reiterated with a note of irascibility. "Who?"

The little voice laughed. "Why! I'm Marjorie!" it said.

Then she was back in his life like a lantern suddenly become visible in a wood at midnight.

It was like meeting her as a china figure, neat and perfect and two inches high. It was her voice, very clear and very bright, and quite characteristic, as though he was hearing it through the wrong end of a telescope. It was her voice, clear as a bell; confident without a shadow.

"It's me! Marjorie! I'm twenty-one to-day!"

It was like a little arrow of exquisite light shot into the very heart of his life.

He laughed back. "Are you for meeting me then, Marjorie?"

<h3 style="text-align:center">§ 4</h3>

They met in Kensington Gardens with an air of being clandestine and defiant. It was one of those days of amber sunlight, soft air, and tender beauty with which London relieves the tragic glooms of the year's decline. There were still a residue of warm-tinted leaves in puffs and clusters upon the tree branches, a boat or two ruffled the blue Serpentine, and the waterfowl gave colour and animation to the selvage of the water. The sedges were still a greenish yellow.

The two met shyly. They were both a little unfamiliar to each other. Trafford was black-coated, silk-hatted, umbrella-d, a decorous young professor in the place of the cheerful aeronaut who had fallen so gaily out of the sky. Marjorie had a new tailor-made dress of russet-green, and a little cloth toque ruled and disciplined the hair he had known as a ruddy confusion.... They had dreamt, I think, of extended arms and a wild rush to embrace one another. Instead, they shook hands.

"And so," said Trafford, "we meet again!"

"I don't see why we shouldn't meet!" said Marjorie.

There was a slight pause.

"Let's have two of those jolly little green chairs," said Trafford....

They walked across the grass towards the chairs he had indicated, and both were full of the momentous things they were finding it impossible to say.

"There ought to be squirrels here, as there are in New York," he said at last.

They sat down. There was a moment's silence, and then Trafford's spirit rose in rebellion and he plunged at this—this stranger beside him.

"Look here," he said, "do you still love me, Marjorie?"

She looked up into his face with eyes in which surprise and scrutiny passed into something altogether beautiful. "I love you—altogether," she said in a steady, low voice.

And suddenly she was no longer a stranger, but the girl who had flitted to his arms breathless, unhesitating, through the dusk. His blood quickened. He made an awkward gesture as though he arrested an impulse to touch her. "My sweetheart," he said. "My dear one!"

Marjorie's face flashed responses. "It's you," he said.

"Me," she answered.

"Do you remember?"

"Everything!"

"My dear!"

"I want to tell you things," said Marjorie. "What are we to do?"....

He tried afterwards to retrace that conversation. He was chiefly ashamed of his scientific preoccupations during that London interval. He had thought of a thousand things; Marjorie had thought of nothing else but love and him. Her happy assurance, her absolute confidence that his desires would march with hers, reproached and confuted every adverse thought in him as though it was a treachery to love. He had that sense which I suppose comes at times to every man, of entire unworthiness for the straight, unhesitating decision, the clear simplicity of a woman's passion. He had dreamt vaguely, unsubstantially, the while he had arranged his pressures and temperatures and infinitesimal ingredients, and worked with goniometer and trial models and the new calculating machine he had contrived for his research. But she had thought clearly, definitely, fully—of nothing but coming to him. She had thought out everything that bore upon that; reasons for preciptance, reasons for delay, she had weighed the rewards of conformity against the glamour of romance. It became more and more clear to him as they talked, that she was determined to elope with him, to go to Italy, and there have an extraordinarily picturesque and beautiful time. Her definiteness shamed his poverty of anticipation. Her enthusiasm carried him with her. Of course it was so that things must be done....

When at last they parted under the multiplying lamps of the November twilight, he turned his face eastward. He was afraid of his mother's eyes—he scarcely knew why. He walked along Kensington Gore, and the clustering confused lights of street and house, white and golden and orange and pale lilac, the moving lamps and shining glitter of the traffic, the luminous interiors of omnibuses, the reflection of carriage and hoarding, the fading daylight overhead, the phantom trees to the left, the deepening shadows and blacknesses among the houses on his right, the bobbing heads of wayfarers, were just for him the stir and hue and texture of fairyland. All the world was fairyland. He went to his club and dined there, and divided the evening between geography, as it is condensed in Baedeker and Murray on North Italy, Italian Switzerland and the Italian Riviera, and a study of the marriage laws as they are expounded in "Whitaker's Almanac," the "Encyclopædia Britannica," and other convenient works of reference. He replaced the books as he used them, and went at last from the library into the smoking-room, but seeing a man who might talk to him there, he went out at once into the streets, and fetched a wide compass by Baker Street, Oxford Street, and Hyde Park, home.

He was a little astonished at himself and everything.

But it was going to be—splendid.

(What poor things words can be!)

§ 5

He found his mother still up. She had been re-reading "The Old Wives' Tale," and she sat before a ruddy fire in the shadow beyond the lit circle of a green-shaded electric light thinking, with the book put aside. In the dimness above was his father's portrait. "Time you were in bed, mother," he said reprovingly, and kissed her eyebrow and stood above her. "What's the book?" he asked, and picked it up and put it down, forgotten. Their eyes met. She perceived he had something to say; she did not know what. "Where have you been?" she asked.

He told her, and they lapsed into silence. She asked another question and he answered her, and the indifferent conversation ended again. The silence lengthened. Then he plunged: "I wonder, mother, if it would put you out very much if I brought home a wife to you?"

So it had come to this—and she had not seen it coming. She looked into the glowing recesses of the fire before her and controlled her voice by an effort. "I'd be glad for you to do it, dear—if you loved her," she said very quietly. He stared down at her for a moment; then he knelt down beside her and took her hand and kissed it. "My dear," she whispered softly, stroking his head, and her tears came streaming. For a time they said no more.

Presently he put coal on the fire, and then sitting on the hearthrug at her feet and looking away from her into the flames—in an attitude that took her back to his boyhood—he began to tell her brokenly and awkwardly of Marjorie.

"It's so hard, mother, to explain these things," he began. "One doesn't half understand the things that are happening to one. I want to make you in love with her, dear, just as I am. And I don't see how I can."

"Perhaps I shall understand, my dear. Perhaps I shall understand better than you think."

"She's such a beautiful thing—with something about her——. You know those steel blades you can bend back to the hilt—and they're steel! And she's tender. It's as if someone had taken tears, mother, and made a spirit out of them——"

She caressed and stroked his hand. "My dear," she said, "I know."

"And a sort of dancing daring in her eyes."

"Yes," she said. "But tell me where she comes from, and how you met her—and all the circumstantial things that a sensible old woman can understand."

He kissed her hand and sat down beside her, with his shoulder against the arm of her chair, his fingers interlaced about his knee. She could not keep her touch from his hair, and she tried to force back the thought in her mind that all these talks must end, that very soon indeed they would end. And she was glad, full of pride and joy too that her son was a lover after her heart, a clean and simple lover as his father had been before him. He loved this unknown Marjorie, finely, sweetly, bravely, even as she herself could have desired to have been loved. She told herself she did not care very greatly even if this Marjorie should prove unworthy. So long as her son was not unworthy.

He pieced his story together. He gave her a picture of the Popes, Marjorie in her family like a jewel in an ugly setting, so it seemed to him, and the queer dull rage of her father and all that they meant to do. She tried to grasp his perplexities and advise, but chiefly she was filled with the thought that he was in love. If he wanted a girl he should have her, and if he had to take her by force, well, wasn't it his right? She set small store upon the Popes that night—or any circumstances. And since she herself had married on the slightest of security, she was concerned very little that this great adventure was to be attempted on an income of a few hundreds a year. It was outside her philosophy that a wife should be anything but glad to tramp the roads if need be with the man who loved her. He sketched out valiant plans, was for taking Marjorie away in the teeth of all opposition and bringing her back to London. It would have to be done decently, of course, but it would have, he thought, to be done. Mrs. Trafford found the prospect perfect; never before had he sounded and looked so like that dim figure which hung still and sympathetic above them. Ever and again she glanced up at her husband's quiet face....

On one point she was very clear with him.

"You'll live with us, mother?" he said abruptly.

"Not with you. As near as you like. But one house, one woman.... I'll have a little flat of my own—for you both to come to me."

"Oh, nonsense, mother! You'll have to be with us. Living alone, indeed!"

"My dear, I'd prefer a flat of my own. You don't understand—everything. It will be better for all of us like that."

There came a little pause between them, and then her hand was on his head again. "Oh, my dear," she said, "I want you to be happy. And life can be difficult. I won't give a chance—for things to go wrong. You're hers, dear, and you've got to be hers—be each other's altogether. I've watched so many people. And that's the best, the very best you can have. There's just the lovers—the real enduring lovers; and the uncompleted people who've failed to find it."...

<h3 align="center">§ 6</h3>

Trafford's second meeting with Marjorie, which, by the by, happened on the afternoon of the following day, brought them near to conclusive decisions. The stiffness of their first encounter in London had altogether vanished. She was at her prettiest and in the highest spirits—and she didn't care for anything else in the world. A gauzy silk scarf which she had bought and not paid for that day floated atmospherically about her straight trim body; her hair had caught the infection of insurrection and was waving rebelliously about her ears. As he drew near her his grave discretion passed from him as clouds pass from a hillside. She smiled radiantly. He held out both his hands for both of hers, and never did a maiden come so near and yet not get a public and shameless kissing.

One could as soon describe music as tell their conversation. It was a matter of tones and feelings. But the idea of flight together, of the bright awakening in unfamiliar sunshine with none to come between them, had gripped them both. A certain sober gravity of discussion only masked that deeper inebriety. It would be easy for them to get away; he had no lectures until February; he could, he said, make arrangements, leave his research. She dreaded disputation. She was for a simple disappearance, notes on pincushions and defiantly apologetic letters from Boulogne, but his mother's atmosphere had been a gentler one than her home's, with a more powerful disposition to dignity. He still couldn't understand that the cantankerous egotism of Pope was indeed the essential man; it seemed to him a crust of bad manners that reason ought to pierce.

The difference in their atmospheres came out in their talk—in his desire for a handsome and dignified wedding—though the very heavens protested—and her resolve to cut clear of every one, to achieve a sort of gaol delivery of her life, make a new beginning altogether, with the minimum of friction and the maximum of surprise. Unused to fighting, he was magnificently prepared to fight; she, with her intimate knowledge of chronic domestic conflict, was for the evasion of all the bickerings, scoldings, and misrepresentations his challenge would occasion. He thought in his innocence a case could be stated and discussed; but no family discussion she had ever heard had even touched the realities of the issue that occasioned it.

"I don't like this underhand preparation," he said.

"Nor I," she echoed. "But what can one do?"

"Well, oughtn't I to go to your father and give him a chance? Why shouldn't I? It's—the dignified way."

"It won't be dignified for father," said Marjorie, "anyhow."

"But what right has he to object?"

"He isn't going to discuss his rights with you. He will object."

"But why?"

"Oh! because he's started that way. He hit you. I haven't forgotten it. Well, if he goes back on that now——He'd rather die than go back on it. You see, he's ashamed in his heart. It would be like confessing himself wrong not to keep it up that you're the sort of man one hits. He just hates you because he hit you. I haven't been his daughter for twenty-one years for nothing."

"I'm thinking of us," said Trafford. "I don't see we oughtn't to go to him just because he's likely to be—unreasonable."

"My dear, do as you please. He'll forbid and shout, and hit tables until things break. Suppose he locks me up!"

"Oh, Habeas Corpus, and my strong right arm! He's much more likely to turn you out-of-doors."

"Not if he thinks the other will annoy you more. I'll have to bear a storm."

"Not for long."

"He'll bully mother till she cries over me. But do as you please. She'll come and she'll beg me——Do as you please. Perhaps I'm a coward. I'd far rather I could slip away."

Trafford thought for a moment. "I'd far rather you could," he answered, in a voice that spoke of inflexible determinations.

They turned to the things they meant to do. "Italy!" she whispered, "Italy!" Her face was alight with her burning expectation of beauty, of love, of the new heaven and the new earth that lay before them. The intensity of that desire blazing through her seemed to shame his dull discretions. He had to cling to his resolution, lest it should vanish in that contagious intoxication.

"You understand I shall come to your father," he said, as they drew near the gate where it seemed discreet for them to part.

"It will make it harder to get away," she said, with no apparent despondency. "It won't stop us. Oh! do as you please."

She seemed to dismiss the question, and stood hand-in-hand with him in a state of glowing gravity. She wouldn't see him again for four-and-twenty hours. Then a thought came into her head—a point of great practical moment.

"Oh!" she said, "of course, you won't tell father you've seen me."

She met his eye. "Really you mustn't," she said. "You see—he'll make a row with mother for not having watched me better. I don't know what he isn't likely to do. It isn't myself——This is a confidential communication—all this. No one in this world knows I am meeting you. If you must go to him, go to him."

"For myself?"

She nodded, with her open eyes on his—eyes that looked now very blue and very grave, and her lips a little apart.

She surprised him a little, but even this sudden weakness seemed adorable.

"All right," he said.

"You don't think that I'm shirking——?" she asked, a little too eagerly.

"You know your father best," he answered. "I'll tell you all he says and all the terror of him here to-morrow afternoon."

§ 7

In the stillness of the night Trafford found himself thinking over Marjorie; it was a new form of mental exercise, which was destined to play a large part in his existence for many subsequent years. There had come a shadow on his confidence in her. She was a glorious person; she had a kind of fire behind her and in her—shining through her, like the lights in a fire-opal, but——He wished she had not made him promise to conceal their meeting and their close co-operation from her father. Why did she do that? It would spoil his case with her father, and it could forward things for them in no conceivable way. And from that, in some manner too subtle to trace, he found his mind wandering to another problem, which was destined to reappear with a slowly dwindling importance very often in this procedure of thinking over Marjorie in the small hours. It was the riddle—it never came to him in the daytime, but only in those intercalary and detachedly critical periods of thought—why exactly had she engaged herself to Magnet? Why had she? He couldn't imagine himself, in Marjorie's position, doing anything of the sort. Marjorie had ways of her own; she was different.... Well, anyhow, she was splendid and loving and full of courage.... He had got no further than this when at last he fell asleep.

§ 8

Trafford's little attempt to regularise his position was as creditable to him as it was inevitably futile. He sought out 29, Hartstone Square in the morning on his way to his laboratory, and he found it one of a great row of stucco houses each with a portico and a dining-room window on the ground floor, and each with a railed area from which troglodytic servants peeped. Collectively the terrace might claim a certain ugly dignity of restraint, there was none of your Queen Anne nonsense of art or beauty about it, and the narrow height, the subterranean kitchens of each constituent house, told of a steep relentless staircase and the days before the pampering of the lower classes began. The houses formed a square, as if the British square so famous at Waterloo for its dogged resistance to all the forces of the universe had immortalized itself in buildings, and they stared upon a severely railed garden of hardy shrubs and gravel to which the tenants had the inestimable privilege of access. They did not use it much, that was their affair, but at any rate they had keys and a nice sense of rights assured, and at least it kept other people out.

Trafford turned out of a busy high road full of the mixed exhilarating traffic of our time, and came along a quiet street into this place, and it seemed to him he had come into a corner of defence and retreat, into an atmosphere of obstinate and unteachable resistances. But this illusion of conservativism in its last ditch was dispelled altogether in Mr. Pope's portico. Youth flashed out of these solemnities like a dart shot from a cave. Trafford was raising his hand to the solid brass knocker when abruptly it was snatched from his fingers, the door was flung open and a small boy with a number of dirty books in a strap flew out and hit him with projectile violence.

"Blow!" said the young gentleman recoiling, and Trafford recovering said: "Hullo, Theodore!"

"Lord!" said Theodore breathless, "It's you! What a lark! Your name's never mentioned—no how. What did you do?... Wish I could stop and see it! I'm ten minutes late. Ave atque vale. So long!"

He vanished with incredible velocity. And Mr. Trafford was alone in possession of the open doorway except for Toupee, who after a violent outbreak of hostility altered his mind and cringed to his feet in abject and affectionate propitiation. A pseudo-twin appeared, said "Hello!" and vanished, and then he had an instant's vision of Mr. Pope, newspaper in hand, appearing from the dining-room. His expression of surprise changed to malevolence, and he darted back into the room from which he had emerged. Trafford decided to take the advice of a small brass plate on his left hand, and "ring also."

A housemaid came out of the bowels of the earth very promptly and ushered him up two flights of stairs into what was manifestly Mr. Pope's study.

It was a narrow, rather dark room lit by two crimson-curtained windows, and with a gas fire before which Mr. Pope's walking boots were warming for the day. The apartment revealed to Trafford's cursory inspection many of the stigmata of an Englishman of active intelligence and literary tastes. There in the bookcase were the collected works of Scott, a good large illustrated Shakespeare in numerous volumes, and a complete set of bound Punches from the beginning. A pile of back numbers of the Times stood on a cane stool in a corner, and in a little bookcase handy for the occupier of the desk were Whitaker, Wisden and an old peerage. The desk bore traces of recent epistolary activity, and was littered with the printed matter of Aunt Plessington's movements. Two or three recent issues of The Financial Review of Reviews were also visible. About the room hung steel engravings apparently of defunct judges or at any rate of exceedingly grim individuals, and over the mantel were trophies of athletic prowess, a bat witnessing that Mr. Pope had once captained the second eleven at Harrogby.

Mr. Pope entered with a stern expression and a sentence prepared. "Well, sir," he said with a note of ironical affability, "to what may I ascribe this—intrusion?"

Mr. Trafford was about to reply when Mr. Pope interrupted. "Will you be seated," he said, and turned his desk chair about for himself, and occupying it, crossed his legs and pressed the finger tips of his two hands together. "Well, sir?" he said.

Trafford remained standing astraddle over the boots before the gas fire.

"Look here, sir," he said; "I am in love with your daughter. She's one and twenty, and I want to see her—and in fact——" He found it hard to express himself. He could think only of a phrase that sounded ridiculous. "I want—in fact—to pay my addresses to her."

"Well, sir, I don't want you to do so. That is too mild. I object strongly—very strongly. My daughter has been engaged to a very distinguished and able man, and I hope very shortly to hear that that engagement—— Practically it is still going on. I don't want you to intrude upon my daughter further."

"But look here, sir. There's a certain justice—I mean a certain reasonableness——"

Mr. Pope held out an arresting hand. "I don't wish it. Let that be enough."

"Of course it isn't enough. I'm in love with her—and she with me. I'm an entirely reputable and decent person——"

"May I be allowed to judge what is or is not suitable companionship for my daughter—and what may or may not be the present state of her affections?"

"Well, that's rather the point we are discussing. After all, Marjorie isn't a baby. I want to do all this—this affair, openly and properly if I can, but, you know, I mean to marry

Marjorie—anyhow."

"There are two people to consult in that matter."

"I'll take the risk of that."

"Permit me to differ."

A feeling of helplessness came over Trafford. The curious irritation Mr. Pope always roused in him began to get the better of him. His face flushed hotly. "Oh really! really! this is—this is nonsense!" he cried. "I never heard anything so childish and pointless as your objection——"

"Be careful, sir!" cried Mr. Pope, "be careful!"

"I'm going to marry Marjorie."

"If she marries you, sir, she shall never darken my doors again!"

"If you had a thing against me!"

"Haven't I!"

"What have you?"

There was a quite perceptible pause before Pope fired his shot.

"Does any decent man want the name of Trafford associated with his daughter. Trafford! Look at the hoardings, sir!"

A sudden blaze of anger lit Trafford. "My God!" he cried and clenched his fists and seemed for a moment ready to fall upon the man before him. Then he controlled himself by a violent effort. "You believe in that libel on my dead father?" he said, with white lips.

"Has it ever been answered?"

"A hundred times. And anyhow!—Confound it! I don't believe—you believe it. You've raked it up—as an excuse! You want an excuse for your infernal domestic tyranny! That's the truth of it. You can't bear a creature in your household to have a will or preference of her own. I tell you, sir, you are intolerable—intolerable!"

He was shouting, and Pope was standing now and shouting too. "Leave my house, sir. Get out of my house, sir. You come here to insult me, sir!"

A sudden horror of himself and Pope seized the younger man. He stiffened and became silent. Never in his life before had he been in a bawling quarrel. He was amazed and ashamed.

"Leave my house!" cried Pope with an imperious gesture towards the door.

Trafford made an absurd effort to save the situation. "I am sorry, sir, I lost my temper. I had no business to abuse you——"

"You've said enough."

"I apologise for that. I've done what I could to manage things decently."

"Will you go, sir?" threatened Mr. Pope.

"I'm sorry I came," said Trafford.

Mr. Pope took his stand with folded arms and an expression of weary patience.

"I did what I could," said Trafford at the door.

The staircase and passage were deserted. The whole house seemed to have caught from Mr. Pope that same quality of seeing him out....

"Confound it!" said Trafford in the street.

"How on earth did all this happen?"...

He turned eastward, and then realized that work would be impossible that day. He changed his direction for Kensington Gardens, and in the flower-bordered walk near the Albert Memorial he sat down on a chair, and lugged at his moustache and wondered. He was extraordinarily perplexed, as well as ashamed and enraged by this uproar. How had it begun? Of course, he had been stupidly abusive, but the insult to his father had been unendurable. Did a man of Pope's sort quite honestly believe that stuff? If he didn't, he deserved kicking. If he did, of course he was entitled to have it cleared up. But then he wouldn't listen! Was there any case for the man at all? Had he, Trafford, really put the thing so that Pope would listen? He couldn't remember. What was it he had said in reply to Pope? What was it exactly that Pope had said?

It was already vague; it was a confused memory of headlong words and answers; what wasn't vague, what rang in his ears still, was the hoarse discord of two shouting voices.

Could Marjorie have heard?

§ 9

So Marjorie carried her point. She wasn't to be married tamely after the common fashion which trails home and all one's beginnings into the new life. She was to be eloped with, romantically and splendidly, into a glorious new world. She walked on shining clouds, and if she felt some remorse, it was a very tender and satisfactory remorse, and with a clear conviction below it that in the end she would be forgiven.

They made all their arrangements elaborately and carefully. Trafford got a license to marry her; she was to have a new outfit from top to toe to go away with on that eventful day. It accumulated in the shop, and they marked the clothes M.T. She was watched, she imagined, but as her father did not know she had seen Trafford, nothing had been said to her, and no attempt was made to prohibit her going out and coming in. Trafford entered into the conspiracy with a keen interest, a certain amusement, and a queer little feeling of distaste. He hated to hide any act of his from any human being. The very soul of scientific work, you see, is publication. But Marjorie seemed to justify all things, and when his soul turned against furtiveness, he reminded it that the alternative was bawling.

One eventful afternoon he went to the college, and Marjorie slipped round by his arrangement to have tea with Mrs. Trafford....

He returned about seven in a state of nervous apprehension; came upstairs two steps at a time, and stopped breathless on the landing. He gulped as he came in, and his eyes were painfully eager. "She's been?" he asked.

But Marjorie had won Mrs. Trafford.

"She's been," she answered. "Yes, she's all right, my dear."

"Oh, mother!" he said.

"She's a beautiful creature, dear—and such a child! Oh! such a child! And God bless you, dear, God bless you....

"I think all young people are children. I want to take you both in my arms and save you.... I'm talking nonsense, dear."

He kissed her, and she clung to him as if he were something too precious to release.

§ 10

The elopement was a little complicated by a surprise manœuvre of Mrs. Pope's. She was more alive to the quality of the situation, poor lady! than her daughter suspected; she was watching, dreading, perhaps even furtively sympathizing and trying to arrange—oh! trying dreadfully to arrange. She had an instinctive understanding of the deep blue quiet in Marjorie's eyes, and the girl's unusual tenderness with Daffy and the children. She peeped under the blind as Marjorie went out, noted the care in her dress, watched her face as she returned, never plumbed her with a question for fear of the answer. She did not dare to breathe a hint of her suspicions to her husband, but she felt things were adrift in swift, smooth water, and all her soul cried out for delay. So presently there came a letter from Cousin Susan Pendexter at Plymouth. The weather was beautiful, Marjorie must come at once, pack up and come and snatch the last best glow of the dying autumn away there in the west. Marjorie's jerry-built excuses, her manifest chagrin and reluctance, confirmed her mother's worst suspicions.

She submitted and went, and Mrs. Pope and Syd saw her off.

I do not like to tell how a week later Marjorie explained herself and her dressing-bag and a few small articles back to London from Plymouth. Suffice it that she lied desperately and elaborately. Her mother had never achieved such miracles of mis-statement, and she added a vigour that was all her own. It is easier to sympathize with her than exonerate her. She was in a state of intense impatience, and—what is strange—extraordinarily afraid that something would separate her from her lover if she did not secure him. She was in a fever of determination.

She could not eat or sleep or attend to anything whatever; she was occupied altogether with the thought of assuring herself to Trafford. He towered in her waking vision over town and land and sea.

He didn't hear the lies she told; he only knew she was magnificently coming back to him. He met her at Paddington, a white-faced, tired, splendidly resolute girl, and they went to the waiting registrar's forthwith.

She bore herself with the intentness and dignity of one who is taking the cardinal step in life. They kissed as though it was a symbol, and were keenly business-like about cabs and luggage and trains. At last they were alone in the train together. They stared at one another.

"We've done it, Mrs. Trafford!" said Trafford.

She snapped like an over-taut string, crumpled, clung to him, and without a word was weeping passionately in his arms.

It surprised him that she could weep as she did, and still more to see her as she walked by his side along the Folkestone pier, altogether recovered, erect, a little flushed and excited like a child. She seemed to miss nothing. "Oh, smell the sea!" she said, "Look at the lights! Listen to the swish of the water below." She watched the luggage spinning on the wire rope of the giant crane, and he watched her face and thought how beautiful she was. He wondered why her eyes could sometimes be so blue and sometimes dark as night.

The boat cleared the pier and turned about and headed for France. They walked the upper deck together and stood side by side, she very close to him.

"I've never crossed the sea before," she said.

"Old England," she whispered. "It's like leaving a nest. A little row of lights and that's all the world I've ever known, shrunken to that already."

Presently they went forward and peered into the night.

"Look!" she said. "Italy! There's sunshine and all sorts of beautiful things ahead. Warm sunshine, wonderful old ruins, green lizards...." She paused and whispered almost noiselessly: "love——"

They pressed against each other.

"And yet isn't it strange? All you can see is darkness, and clouds—and big waves that hiss as they come near...."

§ 11

Italy gave all her best to welcome them. It was a late year, a golden autumn, with skies of such blue as Marjorie had never seen before. They stayed at first in a pretty little Italian hotel with a garden on the lake, and later they walked over Salvator to Morcote and by boat to Ponte Tresa, and thence they had the most wonderful and beautiful tramp in the world to Luino, over the hills by Castelrotto. To the left of them all day was a broad valley with low-lying villages swimming in a luminous mist, to the right were purple mountains. They passed through paved streets with houses the colour of flesh and ivory, with balconies hung with corn and gourds, with tall church campaniles rising high, and great archways giving upon the blue lowlands; they tramped along avenues of sweet chestnut and between stretches of exuberant vineyard, in which men and women were gathering grapes—purple grapes, a hatful for a soldo, that rasped the tongue. Everything was strange and wonderful to Marjorie's eyes; now it would be a wayside shrine and now a yoke of soft-going, dewlapped oxen, now a chapel hung about with ex votos, and now some unfamiliar cultivation—or a gipsy-eyed child—or a scorpion that scuttled in the dust. The very names of the villages were like jewels to her, Varasca, Croglio, Ronca, Sesia, Monteggio. They walked, or sat by the wayside and talked, or rested at the friendly table of some kindly albergo. A woman as beautiful as Ceres, with a white neck all open, made them an omelette, and then fetched her baby from its cradle to nurse it while she talked to them as they made their meal. And afterwards she filled their pockets with roasted chestnuts, and sent them with melodious good wishes upon their way. And always high over all against the translucent blue hung the white shape of Monte Rosa, that warmed in colour as the evening came.

Marjorie's head was swimming with happiness and beauty, and with every fresh delight she recurred again to the crowning marvel of this clean-limbed man beside her, who smiled and carried all her luggage in a huge rucksack that did not seem to exist for him, and watched her and caressed her—and was hers, hers!

At Baveno there were letters. They sat at a little table outside a café and read them, suddenly mindful of England again. Incipient forgiveness showed through Mrs. Pope's reproaches, and there was also a simple, tender love-letter (there is no other word for it) from old Mrs. Trafford to her son.

From Baveno they set off up Monte Mottarone—whence one may see the Alps from Visto to Ortler Spitz—trusting to find the inn still open, and if it was closed to get down to Orta somehow before night. Or at the worst sleep upon the mountain side.

(Monte Mottarone! Just for a moment taste the sweet Italian name upon your lips.) These were the days before the funicular from Stresa, when one trudged up a rude path through the chestnuts and walnuts.

As they ascended the long windings through the woods, they met an old poet and his wife, coming down from sunset and sunrise. There was a word or two about the inn, and they went upon their way. The old man turned ever and again to look at them.

"Adorable young people," he said. "Adorable happy young people....

"Did you notice, dear, how she held that dainty little chin of hers?...

"Pride is such a good thing, my dear, clear, straight pride like theirs—and they were both so proud!...

"Isn't it good, dear, to think that once you and I may have looked like that to some passer-by. I wish I could bless them—sweet, swift young things! I wish, dear, it was possible for old men to bless young people without seeming to set up for saints...."